Jinx

Cara R. Newman

ISBN: 1511441364
ISBN-13: 978-1511441360

DEDICATION

For my family

CONTENTS

ACKNOWLEDGMENTS

I'd like to thank my mother, my father and my grandmother for helping me think through all of my ideas and help me edit and revise my story.

Prologue

Two magicians crept through the woods. They were husband and wife. The wife, Alexis, carried a newborn baby in her arms. It was her baby. The baby looked adorable in her pink pajamas that her mother had made out of flower petals using her magic.

Now, these two magicians don't just know some silly fake magic tricks. They know real magic. Alexis used to be a tiny fairy, who was the size of a bumblebee. However, she got bigger with the help of another fairy's magic. Alexis had also magically made her wings disappear. Alexis had loved her life as a fairy, but she wanted to be a magician with her husband, James, much, much more.

James used to be a wizard in the magical world. He wore a painted blue hat with yellow stars and he also often wore a matching robe. But, he had given it up to be a magician in the non-magical world with Alexis.

Finally, the magicians found what they were looking for, a house in the woods. They had been watching this house since they found out that Alexis was pregnant, hoping that this would be the perfect place for their daughter to grow up. Their hope was that this house would hide her from any evil, jealous wizards or fairies who would try to steal her powers or even kill her.

Alexis and James tried to hold back their tears as they were about to give away their baby forever. The only place they would see her again was through their crystal ball, but their baby would not be able to see them. They gave her one last hug and left her on the porch of the house. They rang the doorbell and ran from the house crying, leaving the new parents with little information, only a bracelet with her birth date and her name, Jinx.

Five Years Later

Jinx was five years old. She had just started kindergarten

and she still had no idea that her adopted mother and father were not her real parents. Even Kate and Jack, Jinx's adopted parents, did not know where Jinx came from. They had loved her as if she was their own daughter since the day they had answered the door and found her on their porch.

Jinx loved magic, but she still needed to learn that things like going to the bathroom are not real magic. Her true parents, Alexis and James, were becoming more and more famous every year and Jinx was a huge fan. She even had a backpack with pictures of them on it and her room was full of posters of them. Jinx looked like a mini-Alexis with her beautiful long, blonde hair, neon green eyes, long eyelashes, pale skin and rosy cheeks. However, Jinx had never noticed.

One day, as Jinx was pretending to turn her dog, Zully, into a pineapple with her play magician set, the doorbell rang. Jinx ran to the door to see who it was since they rarely had visitors. But, there was no one outside. Jinx looked around and noticed a wooden basket sitting on the porch. There was a purple, polka-dotted blanket inside. Jinx was curious so she carefully and slowly lifted up the blanket and saw a baby. The baby had pale skin with neon green eyes and little sprouts of blonde hair. When Jinx looked into the baby's eyes, the baby started to cry. Jinx noticed a shimmering bracelet on the baby's wrist that read, Trix. Jinx looked around to see who might have brought this baby to her home. She only saw two dark shadows moving quickly into the woods.

Jinx picked up the basket with the baby, turned and went inside her house, calling, "Mommy, I got a baby!"

Her parents raced to the door. They took one look at the basket with the baby inside and stared at each other.

"I got it from the porch," said Jinx, excitedly. "I always thought babies came from mommys!"

Chapter 1
The Glowing Letter

"Taa-daa!" Jinx screamed over the cheering crowd.

"Thank you!" roared her sister, Trix.

The audience of teddy bears and dolls came to a slow stop from applauding in both of the sisters' imaginations.

"I think we are ready to show Mommy and Daddy!" squeaked five year old Trix.

The two sisters shoved and pushed, trying to get ahead of the other to tell their mother and father about the magic show first. In the end, Jinx, who was almost five years older than her sister, won? "Can we...show you...our," she panted.

"Magic show!" interrupted Trix, knocking Jinx to the floor.

"Sure," said their father, Jack, putting down the newspaper and helping Jinx back up to her feet.

"Jack, the last time they did this they started a fire," their mother, Kate complained.

"Please," Jinx pleaded. "We're older now!"

"Please, please, please, please!" Trix begged.

"Fine," Kate sighed sitting on the floor and pushing her overgrown bangs out of her face.

Jinx and Trix waited for their father to join their mother on the floor. As Jack did this, Jinx, who was now taller than him could see a big bald patch surrounded by Jack's shaggy black hair. He sat there, smiling up at them, his forehead wrinkling, as he waited for his daughters to start.

"Welcome to our magic show!" Jinx announced.

"Starring the awesome Trix!" shouted Trix.

"And the magnificent Jinx," Jinx added jumping in front of Trix. "Our first trick will be making a tadpole turn into a frog in only thirty seconds!"

“Hold on a minute,” Trix said excitedly.

Jinx and Trix stumbled up the stairs to get their supplies. After that, they both almost stumbled back down the stairs carrying a fake wand, an empty cup and a tank with their pet frog, Lily, and their pet tadpole, Pad.

While hiding their supplies, Jinx sat down with her back to her parents and put everything on the floor. Trix sat down too and picked up the empty cup. She dunked the cup into the water and swished it around until she caught Lily. She scooped Lily up with some extra water. Jinx picked up the tank that now only had Pad in it and motioned for Trix to stay hiding Lily.

“Here it goes,” she said turning around and revealing herself and Pad to her parents. “Please close your eyes as we do the trick.”

Suddenly, the doorbell rang. This hardly ever happened in their medium sized house in the woods because no one could ever find it. The last time the doorbell had rung was when Trix had been delivered. However, Jinx had been told that had been all her imagination. Now, Jinx and Trix raced to the door and tugged it open.

Standing on the door step was a very odd woman from head to toe. She was short and very skinny. However, those were the only normal things about her. Her grayish hair stuck straight above her head about a foot. She had dark green eyes with extremely long lashes which gave her a cat-like look. Her ears were slightly pointed and almost a little like an elf's. Her yellowing teeth were crooked. She wore a long black cape with a black and purple striped dress. One of her shoes was pointed and looked like something an elf might wear while her other shoe had a high heel and seemed expensive. Her fingernails were painted purple and were so long that they were starting to curl.

Trix and Jinx jumped aside. They forgot about the magic show. They forgot they were in magician costumes and Jinx forgot she was holding a fake magic wand.

"Hello," the odd woman snarled. "What are your names?"

"I'm not allowed to talk to strangers!" Jinx shouted bravely back at her.

"Especially ugly ones like you," Trix added taking a step backwards.

Suddenly, the odd woman fell to her knees and put

her hand over her chest. Kate and Jack came over to the door wondering what was going on and looked at each other with confused expressions.

Just as Jack was about to ask what was going on, out of nowhere came five pale creatures. They could not have been more than a foot and a half tall. The creatures were completely bald and wore purple suits with pointed black shoes. They looked just as scared as Jinx and her family. They slowly circled around the odd lady and somehow managed to pick her up. As they carried her out of the house, Jinx, Trix, Kate and Jack each stared at one another, with their jaws dropped open and their eyes about to pop out of their heads.

The next day was a school day for Jinx. When the bell rang at the end of the day, she ran through the forest to her house. Usually, she would stroll through the forest, listening to the birds chirp, or in winter, like it was now, trying to walk silently so she could hear an animal trot through the snow. But today, she could not keep her mind off the odd lady. She kept feeling like the strange woman and those creatures were watching her. She wanted to get home as fast as possible so she would be safe.

She arrived at her house in record time. She checked the mailbox which like the doorbell had hardly ever been used. Mailmen usually gave up trying to find their house. Jinx figured it was useless to check the mail, but she was hoping to receive a letter from her best friend, Lola. Lola had mysteriously vanished on her 10th birthday and Jinx kept hoping to hear something from her. Unfortunately, there was nothing there. Jinx slumped to the door of her house.

Just as she was about to open the door, a blinding light from behind her, startled her. The light was coming from the mailbox. Jinx thought that it was probably not a good idea to check out what was causing the light as she remembered what had happened just the day before when she had answered the door. However, her curiosity took over. Running cautiously, she raced back to the mailbox and swung the door open. She reached her hand inside and touched an envelope. As soon as she touched it, the light died down. Jinx pulled it out and looked at it. The envelope was gold and was addressed to Jinx's parents, Mr. and Mrs. Watson. There was no return address. Without giving it too much thought or thinking of how much trouble she could get into, Jinx tore the envelope open as quickly as she could with her mittens on. She unfolded the paper inside and read:

Dear Mr. and Mrs. Watson,

First of all, we would like to thank you from the bottom of our hearts for taking such good care of our daughters. We would have loved to raise them ourselves and have missed them so much, but have been comforted by what we have seen in our crystal ball. You have given them such love and happiness.

What we have to tell you is very surprising and complicated news. Tomorrow will be Jinx's 10th birthday. As her true mother and father, we would like her to be prepared for the unexpected things we see coming through our crystal ball. There will be many magical things happening. Tomorrow, Jinx will become the most powerful sorcerer on earth. This means the current most powerful sorcerer, who has kept herself alive for the past 2,036 years will lose her power in the following month and die. This sorcerer will do everything in her power to kill Jinx. Sometime, in the next three days, Jinx's grandmother will arrive to explain more. This is all we can say in a letter. Please remember to warn Jinx.

Sincerely,

Alexis and James Silverspark

Chapter 2
The Dark Side

The most powerful, dangerous sorcerer trotted deeper and deeper into the woods. She was known as Wazilma by every sorcerer in every country in the magical world and they only knew her as Wazilma, not as any of the other mysterious people she used as disguises.

"Gikamin!" she bellowed at her most loyal assistant.

"Wazilma?" Gikamin asked looking her over. "Who are you?"

"I am Wazilma!" Wazilma snarled. "I stopped myself in the middle of a transformation."

"So that's why you're wearing two different shoes?" Gikamin asked bursting into laughter.

Wazilma shot Gikamin a nasty look before waving her wand to finish her transformation. This version of Wazilma had curly black hair that went all the way down her back. Her clothes remained the same, with a long black cape and black and purple striped dress. However, she wore two high heeled shoes. She wore a black short top hat with a veil in the front that covered half of her face and she was extremely tall and very skinny giving her a skeletal appearance.

"You little elves," Wazilma growled. "You're such – well, tiny and weird!"

"Hey! You are a..." started Gikamin

"Shhh," Wazilma interrupted putting her finger over her lips. "I never want to hear that spoken aloud. And if I hear that you do, you are dead!"

Gikamin nervously changed the subject and asked, "So was it her? Was it Jinx? Did you kill her? You're running out of time. You have been searching for ten years! I don't think you'll have any time to find her if this wasn't her."

"Shush. No, no, and no," Wazilma replied. "She didn't answer when I asked her name and there were two of them. Two girls. However, they both seemed to know they are sorcerers. They were wearing magician clothes and one was even holding a wand. The younger one insulted me deeply and you know I have no tolerance for insults!"

"How do you know the clothes and wands were real?" Gikamin wondered aloud.

"Well," said Wazilma thinking. "I don't know for sure now that you mention it. I had to make an unexpected hasty exit. Why don't we find out for sure?"

"We?" Gikamin asked nervously.

"Oh, did I say we?" Wazilma scowled. "I meant you. Now go run back there and bring me the older girl!"

Gikamin turned so pale that he looked white and every inch of his body was trembling. "Where is the house? What if I get eaten by a fox or something even worse?"

"You'll find the house, hopefully," Wazilma said smirking. "If you are not back in an hour, I'll send another elf." Gikamin sighed with relief. Wazilma snarled at him, "Not to save you. To finish the job!"

"What if I die? I'm your most loyal assistant." whined Gikamin.

"I'll get another one," Wazilma replied. She cackled

and shooed Gikamin into the forest. "Don't forget this!" she called after him picking up his wand and throwing it at him. Gikamin caught his wand in the air and took off at full speed. Wazilma went into her fake log cabin in the woods and through the portal into her mansion.

Gikamin ran faster than he ever had. He kept going until up ahead he noticed a dog running straight at him. The dog got closer and closer to him until he was only about a foot away. Before Gikamin thought about using his wand to protect himself from the dog, Gikamin jumped and landed right on the dog's back. Gikamin turned around on the dog's back so he could look forward and grabbed onto the dog's ears before he fell off since the dog never even slowed down. Gikamin was so small and light, the large dog didn't even seem to notice him.

Before long, Gikamin spotted something in the distance. As they got closer, he was able to tell that it was a house. The dog seemed to be heading straight towards it. When they reached the house, the dog came to a halt right at the doorstep. Gikamin hopped off the dog's back and the dog began to scratch at the front door. Gikamin pulled out his wand and started to think of a spell that would open the door.

"I lost my keys, don't know where they went, please open the door for me," Gikamin chanted as he waved his wand at the door. Nothing happened.

"Who's there?" asked the dog turning around. The dog was obviously a girl because of her high pitched voice.

Gikamin jumped. He had seen boliquas (magical creatures that did not speak) talk before but that was only because Wazilma had put a spell on them giving them the ability to speak.

"Go away!" screeched the dog.

"I'm just an elf," cried Gikamin.

"Are you on the dark side?" asked the dog.

"No!" lied Gikamin. "I just came to warn Jinx and her family about Wazilma. I only want to help them. I am Gik –kie." Gikamin was afraid the dog may have heard his name on the dark side.

"I'm Zully," the dog said. "I got lost one day a long time ago and just now finally found my way back to my owners," she added waving her paw at the house. "Do you not keep up with current sorcerer news? Of course, that spell isn't going to work. You aren't doing it right."

Gikamin looked at the dog questioningly. "What are you talking about?"

Zully answered, "Well, for starters, it doesn't even rhyme. And, I've read in some sorcerer newspaper that if it is not a very powerful spell, you only have to imagine what you want clearly and wave your wand twice about your head to make it happen. It is hard though because not everyone can picture it very clearly. And it depends on how powerful a sorcerer you are."

Suddenly, the front door opened interrupting the elf and the dog. A woman with long bangs and her brown hair tied back in a ponytail, stepped out. Before Zully or the woman could react, Gikamin did. He was guessing this was Jinx, so he quickly imagined the woman tied up in a black bag and he waved his wand twice around his head. Luckily for him, he was much better at this kind of spell and a big black bag instantly fell over the woman's head. She fell to the ground and a rope tied it shut at the end. Gikamin snatched the bag up and ran into the bushes with the bag over his shoulder.

"Liar!" Zully called into the bushes as she ran after Gikamin. The bushes were very prickly and thorns started scratching her skin underneath her shaggy coat of golden fur. The thorns were not good for Gikamin either. They kept pricking holes in the black bag. However, they did help the woman as the holes made it easier for her to breathe.

Unfortunately, Zully could not handle the thorns

anymore and she had to end her chase. She stepped out of the bushes planning on heading back to the house.

The bag was getting very heavy for little Gikamin, but he kept moving through the woods. After more than an hour, another elf appeared in the bushes. "Gisheramit!" Gikamin called. Gisheramit was another elf and also Gikamin's older brother. Gisheramit was much stronger than Gikamin. His purple suit was very tight due to his large muscles whereas Gikamin was so skinny he was always afraid his pants were going to fall down.

Gisheramit grabbed the other side of the bag and they set off into the forest going three times faster than before.

"I'm glad you are safe," said Gisheramit.

"Me, too," said Gikamin feeling much safer next to his brother.

"Are you sure this is the girl?" asked Gisheramit. "She seems pretty big for a ten year old."

Gikamin shrugged. Inside, he started to doubt himself. *The girl in the bag certainly seems much bigger than a ten year old*, Gikamin thought. But it had been a long time since he had been around humans, so he just shrugged again.

"Well, let's hope it is because Wazilma is probably going to go crazy and kill both of us if you got the wrong girl!" Gisheramit warned him. Gikamin no longer felt safe. He was definitely not sure of himself and he felt his entire body start to shake with fear.

"Are you okay?" asked Gisheramit. "What happened at the house?"

"Before I even found the house, I was running through the woods and I ran into a dog..." By the time Gikamin finished the story, they were inside the portal to Wazilma's mansion.

"That's some imagination you've got there. A talking dog? That spell is against the law! They say it is not natural," Gisheramit explained.

"We are on the dark side, Gisheramit!" squeaked Gikamin. "We break laws all the time! Wazilma uses that spell with the boliquas all the time when she needs them to speak!"

"Yes, but you know how Wazilma is!" Gisheramit whispered as they stepped out of the portal. "And right now we have more important things to worry about than a talking dog, like whether the right girl is in the bag!"

Gikamin gulped.

Chapter 3
The Locked Portal

Jinx almost fainted as she finished rereading the letter for the second time. *Is this good news or bad news*, she wondered. Something suddenly caught her eye. There was something big and black moving through the bushes. As she was wondering what it was, something else emerged out of the bushes. It was big, but golden. It took Jinx no longer than a second to recognize that it was her lost dog, Zully.

A few years ago, Jinx had been playing with Zully outside her house. Zully had spotted a squirrel heading into the forest and before Jinx could stop her, Zully chased the squirrel into the forest. Jinx and her parents had tried to look for her, but hadn't been able to find her.

Zully and Jinx took steps towards each other and stared into each other's eyes. *Is this really Zully? How had she found her way back?* Jinx wondered. *Why is she staring like that? Why is her expression so...human-like?*

There was a long silence. Jinx did not talk and Zully did not bark. Zully was the first to break the silence, calmly saying, "So have you missed me?"

Jinx jumped backwards and fell into the snow. She stared at Zully as though Zully was an alien. Jinx was speechless. "I just imagined that. I've been told many times I have a big imagination," she whispered to herself.

"I said, did you miss me?" Zully repeated loudly and clearly.

"Yes!" Jinx said still in shock and then everything went black.

Jinx opened her eyes and looked around. Zully was standing directly over her. She started barking and then slowly changed her barks into speech. "I missed you too!" Zully bent down and gave Jinx a slobbery lick on the cheek. "You fainted. Sorry! I thought you believed in magic," the dog whimpered looking at her front paws.

"I do believe in magic. I guess I was surprised," Jinx

said truthfully. “And I forgive you. I know you didn’t mean to make me faint.”

“She forgives me! She forgives me!” Zully shouted happily.

“Shh!” whispered Jinx. “I don’t want my mom to hear.”

“Your mom won’t hear me all the way over here,” Zully said doubtfully shaking her head.

“Why?” Jinx questioned.

“Because she’s deep in the forest,” Zully replied.

“Why?” repeated Jinx.

“Because she was kidnapped by an elf who works for Wazilma,” Zully answered casually like it was normal for your mother to be kidnapped by an imaginary creature who works for someone with a strange, kind of scary name.

“What?” yelled Jinx. “First, the craziness yesterday, and then I get a letter from people, who say they are my parents, then you are back and you talk and now my mom is kidnapped by an elf or at least the person who I always thought was my mom! What is going on?”

“Calm down, Jinx. It’s going to be okay. I know…”

"Why? Why?" Jinx wondered out loud. "I've always wanted magic to happen, but never where my mom gets kidnapped!"

"Your mom was kidnapped because the elf thought it was you, I'm guessing," Zully said quickly so she could not be interrupted.

"Hold on! Wazilma must be the evil and most powerful sorcerer this letter warned me about!" Jinx said shaking the letter she was still holding. Then a worried expression appeared on her face, "And she's got my mom."

"Jinx, it'll be okay. I know where your mom is. We'll find her together. Follow me."

Jinx hugged Zully then asked, "How do you know all this stuff?"

Zully gave a weird shrug and replied, "When you wander in the forest for five years, you overhear lots of things."

Just when Jinx was about to ask how Zully could talk, Zully took off into the forest and called, "Follow me!"

Jinx took off after Zully running faster than she ever had. She needed to rescue her mom as fast as possible.

Zully slowed down and stopped. When Jinx caught up and stopped next to Zully, Zully said, “Hop on my back!”

Jinx refused to hop on, “No! I’m too heavy!”

“It’s okay. I’m very strong from years of running around the forest,” Zully encouraged. But Jinx stood where she was and did not move. She had made her decision and did not get on until Zully scurried underneath Jinx’s legs and picked her up.

“You’re going to get hurt!” Jinx cried.

Zully ignored her. She ran deeper and deeper, going faster and faster into the forest. Jinx looked around her. She had never been so deep. The trees were barely inches apart and Jinx wondered how Zully was making it through the trees. There was no sign of sunlight all around them.

Suddenly, Zully stopped. They could hear snow crunching ahead. A light was also shining ahead of them. Jinx climbed off Zully. She could see about a dozen tiny shadowy figures standing in a line before the glowing light. Jinx squinted trying to make out what the figures could be. The shadowy figures and the light moved toward an empty patch of ground and into a small cabin. As the light went into the cabin too, Jinx noticed that the light was an animal. She didn’t recognize it as it was not an animal you would see in a zoo. It had hands and feet, however, it seemed to be walking on its hands. Its face was in the center of its stomach and was surrounded by what looked like needles.

"What is that ugly creature?" Jinx asked.

"A boliqua," answered Zully. Zully looked at Jinx and saw her confused expression, so he added, "A magical animal. It glows in the dark."

"Oh," said Jinx still very confused. "So where is my mom?"

"The hut," replied Zully.

Zully and Jinx crept towards the cabin together and peeked into one of the windows trying to be as silent as possible to not attract any attention. Inside the hut, they saw the boliqua and the dozen creatures which Jinx realized were the same little things who had carried the odd lady away from her house the day before. They all stood huddled together in the center of the cabin and appeared to be waiting for something.

"Elves," whispered Zully feeling that Jinx was going to ask more questions.

An elf stepped forward. A small purple circle

appeared in midair. It started making circles getting bigger and bigger. The elf jumped into the now enormous purple circle and disappeared. The rest of the elves and the boliqua jumped into the purple circle too and vanished.

Zully and Jinx entered into the hut which was now empty. They looked around them and saw only four wooden walls and an empty room. The two of them stared at the purple circle in front of them.

"It's a portal," explained Zully. "That's where your mom is, on the other side of the portal."

"Are you sure?" asked Jinx feeling nervous.

"Those elves work for Wazilma, the woman who stole your mother," answered Zully.

"Oh," said Jinx, trying to look less confused than she was.

"On the count of three, jump," Zully told her. "One...two...three!" Jinx and Zully both tried to jump into the circle as they had just watched the elves and the boliqua do. However, as soon as they hit the circle, they were both knocked to the floor.

"What?" asked Jinx. "How could they get through?"

"Good question," said a mysterious voice.

"Who's there?" Zully shouted, guarding Jinx. Zully's shouts echoed through the cabin.

"Me," said the voice as a ghostly face appeared in the portal, "to answer your questions, little girl."

"I'm not little!" Jinx shouted.

"Calm down, little girl. I won't hurt you," said the ghost-like face smirking. "Now, to answer your question, only trained sorcerers can get through this portal. This is a locked portal. You, little girl, are a sorcerer, not yet trained, and you, doggy –"

Now, it was Zully's turn to be angry. "Don't call me doggy!" she shouted at the face.

But, the ghostly face ignored her and carried on, "Doggy, you're just a normal dog who has been cursed by accident by the Evil One!" the face cackled and echoed several times before dying down.

"Stop making up these ridiculous stories!" bellowed Zully.

"Oh, these aren't fake. You should remember being cursed, doggy," the face sneered. "It's my job to identify everyone who comes here, even if they have no identity, such as you two!"

Jinx stared at the face trying to think of something mean she could say or do to the odd face. Since she couldn't think of anything, she made the ugliest face she could and glared at him. Zully, who still stood on guard, seemed to be thinking the same thing. However, she appeared to be able to think of something to do. Zully was a strong dog who had survived alone in the forest for years. She had fought off things twice as big as her. Right now, she was ready to attack. Zully waited for when it would be least expected. The time had come. The face was smirking at Jinx, proud of the mean things he had said. Zully leaped forward, but she wasn't strong enough to break through the portal and she fell hard onto the floor. She whimpered.

Jinx rushed to Zully's side. "Are you okay? Does it hurt anywhere?"

Zully was too focused on the face to talk, so instead she gently waved her front paw.

"Oh, you want to fight? Dog versus ghost? Sure!" the face teased as he floated out of the portal. Zully whimpered again.

"I'll do it!" Jinx announced. "I'll fight!"

"Don't do it!" Zully begged. "Please!"

Jinx ignored her. She stepped forward making fists

with her hands and she punched at the face. However, the face moved.

"Ha! Missed me! Missed me!" The face was laughing and seemed to be enjoying himself greatly. "Oooh, you missed me!"

Jinx panted. She was so tired. She wanted to fall asleep, but she wouldn't give up. She was going to get her mom back or die trying.

The face suddenly stopped in the middle of the room and said, "Come on, little girl! Is that the best you can do?"

Jinx slowly stepped forward. She looked back at her whimpering dog and then back at the face. She smacked the face as hard as she could, but she did not touch the face...her hand went right through it. She stared at her hand. Nothing was there except a thick coat of goo. "Ew!" she screamed.

"Ha ha! I got you! I won the fight! I won the fight!" the face bragged. He stared down at Jinx as she tried to wipe the goo off her hand. Then, the face stopped his bragging and said more seriously, "Oh my, I'm identifying something here."

"Oh, great! Another one of your stories!" said Zully

sarcastically.

"It's her! It's her! It's Jinx! Wazy come here!" the face shouted.

"Ditty! How many times have I told you not to call me Wazy! I've also told you not to lie!" called a voice from the other end of the portal.

"I'm not lying Wazilma!" Ditty called back.

"Oh no! Wazilma is coming! She's the evil one your true parents warned you about," whispered Zully forgetting about her injury and getting up on her paws. "Hop on!" This time, Jinx did not complain. She knew Zully was injured and she would be in a lot of pain, but they both would be in danger if they stayed any longer. Zully took off out of the hut and disappeared back into the miles of trees. They could hear Wazilma shrieking in the cabin at Ditty, "Liar! Liar!"

"How do you know what the letter says?" Jinx asked Zully as they were racing through the trees.

"I read it when you fainted," Zully replied. Zully stopped quickly. Something was standing in front of them. There was a bright light.

"Is it a boliqua?" whispered Jinx.

"I don't think so," Zully answered as a thick beam of

light rose into their eyes.

Jinx squinted to see who or what was there. A person stood in front of them with a shiny stick in her hand.

"Hello," said the woman excitedly. "You must be Jinx! I'm your grandmother. I'm a wizard."

"I'm your other grandmother," said a squeaky voice from below. Jinx looked down. On her hand, there appeared to be a little bug. Looking closer, Jinx realized it was not a bug, but a tiny person there with wings. It appeared to be a fairy. Jinx's smile spread all over her face.

Chapter 4
The Dawn of Magic

"I have a fairy as a grandmother!" Jinx exclaimed staring at the amazing little fairy in her hand. She had straight, gray hair that brushed her shoulders. She wore a pink dress made of flower petals and her transparent wings were a light shade of blue.

"Don't forget about me! You also have a wizard for a grandmother," reminded her other grandmother sounding slightly annoyed. Jinx took her eyes off her fairy grandmother and gave her attention to her wizard grandmother who was a plump woman with graying, curly hair under a pointed wizard hat. She wore a long night-blue robe covered in tiny yellow stars that matched her hat.

"Oh, I didn't forget," Jinx said excitedly. "What should I call you both?"

"Granny," replied her wizard grandmother.

"Nana," answered her fairy grandmother dreamily, like all anyone would ever want was to be called Nana.

"The letter said that you would be coming!" Jinx whispered happily thinking of her future. "What do you have to warn me about?"

"Well, something strange is going to happen tonight at midnight," Nana whispered, fluttering her wings. "But, no sorcerer is supposed to know about the strange things that are going to happen before they happen."

"Okay," said Jinx still confused and a bit scared. "Can you stay with me tonight, please?"

"Yes, of course," Granny replied excitedly. "We were already planning to stay with you tonight so tomorrow we can bring you to Malunia. Malunia is where we live."

Wow, things were happening so fast. Jinx didn't know whether to be excited about this or not. Then, she remembered her mom and Wazilma and the portal. She asked her grandmothers, "Are you trained sorcerers?"

“Of course,” Nana squeaked. “Why?”

“Because then you can get into the portal to rescue my mom!” Jinx answered sighing with relief.

“What portal?” asked Granny, completely confused.

“Save your mom from what?” questioned Nana, just as confused.

“Alexis is fine. Isn’t she Nana?” wondered Granny turning to look at the tiny fairy.

“My other mother,” corrected Jinx.

“Her adopted mom, the one who has been taking care of her all of these years,” Zully explained.

Granny jumped as she looked at the talking dog. Nana flew into Granny’s curly, gray hair.

“Aren’t you guys used to magic!” Jinx asked them.

“Yes, but the curse on that dog is illegal!” Nana answered flying out of Granny’s hair.

“I’ll tell the story later of how I can speak, but we have something bigger to worry about now,” warned Zully.

“Ok. Fine. But still, what portal and save her from what?” Granny wondered trying to sound calmer than she was.

"The portal in Wazilma's cabin!" Jinx told her.

"We need to save Jinx's mom from Wazilma," added Zully. "I think Wazilma's elves meant to kidnap Jinx, but they took her mom instead."

"Oh no!" Nana cried. "Wazilma must have finally found your parents hiding spot. We were so close to your tenth birthday. We only needed one more day! Unfortunately, we can't save your mom yet. It's too dangerous and Wazilma is still too powerful. Starting tomorrow though, Wazilma will begin to lose her power and Jinx, you will start gaining power as you begin your training. As Wazilma becomes weaker, we will have a better chance rescuing your mom."

"Okay," whispered Jinx softly, a tear falling down her cheek. "After my training, will I be able to do it myself?"

"Yes, after your training. I'm sorry, we can't help you sooner," Granny said sadly.

"Why don't we go to your house, Jinx?" Zully suggested starring up at a now sobbing Jinx.

"Okay," Jinx sniffed.

When they got closer to the house, they could see

the sun starting to set. Jinx saw her father on her front lawn looking very worried. Trix was standing near him. Trix saw the group first and they watched her point them out to her father.

Jack started running towards Jinx shouting, "Where were you? Are you okay? Is your mother with you? Who is this woman and dog with you? There's a strange bug on your head!"

He reached Jinx and gave her a hug as the others all started speaking at once.

"Don't you recognize me, Jack?" Zully asked.

"I'm a wizard!" Granny announced. "I am Jinx's grandmother."

"I'm not a bug! I'm a fairy!" Nana corrected as she flew off Jinx and began to pull what was left of Jinx's father's hair. "Jinx's other grandmother."

"You must be Trix. You're my granddaughter too. You can call me Granny," Granny said looking down at Trix, who looked like a smaller Jinx.

"I'm Nana," Nana told Trix in her dreamy voice.

"Awesome," whispered Trix.

"Fairy! Wizard! Talking dog!" Jinx's father cried

disbelievingly. "I must have hit my head," he said to himself.

"It's fine, Dad. They're –"Jinx started to explain.

"Tell me what happened, Jinx," demanded her father. Jinx and Zully took turns talking as they told her father the entire story from the time Jinx got out of school and found the letter to when she met her grandmothers in the forest.

"Yes, it makes so much more sense now," Jinx's father whispered sarcastically when they finished. "Can I see the letter?" Jinx handed the letter to her father which was crumpled and soggy from her journey through the woods and snow.

Jinx's father read the letter while they all stood quietly waiting. When he finished, he said, "Jinx and Trix, you need to get some sleep. I'm going to talk to your grandmothers. Try not to worry about your mom. We'll figure everything out in the morning."

Jinx didn't remember falling asleep, but suddenly her eyes opened. She stared at the ceiling. She glanced at the clock, three seconds past midnight. It was officially her tenth birthday. She felt something beneath her; it felt like water, clean, warm, water. Jinx floated up out of her bed as a giant golden star grew on each of her legs surrounded by millions of tiny silver stars. Her body turned all silver, then all bronze and then all gold. All of a sudden, the colors shattered and flew into her heart. She drifted to the ground and landed on her feet. However, instead of feeling frightened, Jinx felt more calm and peaceful than she ever had in her life.

She looked back behind her expecting to see the water she had felt, but instead she saw wings attached to her. Before she could think about it much, she felt exhausted and just as suddenly as she had awakened, she was back asleep, on her cozy pink rug, smiling.

With a blanket over her shoulders, to conceal her new wings from her father and Trix, Jinx sat at the kitchen table stuffing her breakfast cereal into her mouth. As she ate the last bite, she jumped up from the table and raced up the stairs, hoping for a few moments to herself to test out her new wings.

"No, no, no, birthday girl, you are not going

anywhere this morning except Malunia," Granny reminded her as her plump body appeared at the top of the stairs. "You need to show them your back, young sorcerer." Granny pointed back down the stairs where Trix and her father were sitting.

"No, I can't," Jinx refused.

"I said, show them your back," Granny repeated.

Jinx, who did not want to argue with her new grandmother, turned and walked back down the stairs. When she entered the kitchen, she removed the blanket to reveal her wings, which grew out of her back and out through holes in her shirt. They were beautiful, sparkly transparent wings.

"They're so pretty! You have wings! Fly! Fly! Fly!" Trix shouted as she walked closer to examine them carefully. "I want some!" she announced.

Jinx looked at her father and surprisingly, he gave her a small smile. "I get it now. Nana and Granny stayed up most of the night to help me understand all of it. It's going to take a lot of getting used to, but I'm trying."

Something caught Jinx eyes as she looked over at Granny. There were silver shimmering stars on Granny's legs. "Granny, what's on your legs?" she asked.

"Silver stars, the symbol of a wizard. Your golden stars show that you are the most powerful sorcerer in the world. Your wings show that you are a fairy. You are the most powerful sorcerer because you have the powers of a fairy and a wizard and no one like that has ever existed. That is why we need you to complete your training, because only you can save your mom and bring an end to Wazilma. "

"Oh," said Jinx feeling overwhelmed.

When Granny left the room, Trix asked, "Can you give me wings?"

Jinx imagined her sister with wings. "I don't know how," she told her. But just as she was saying that, wings started sprouting from her sister's back.

Nana flew into the kitchen, "Jinx what have you done? Be careful with your powers! Anything you think or imagine, if you think it clearly enough, will come true. I guess we should have warned you. You will have to complete six tasks before you are able to fully control your powers. Until then, you must be extremely careful with what you are thinking about." Nana closed her eyes and waved her wand above her head. Trix's wings faded.

Trix sighed. Nana said to her, "On your tenth birthday, you'll get your own pair." Trix smiled and sat on the floor next to Zully who was still asleep.

Zully yawned and said, “Hi Trix. Do you remember me? I got lost in the forest a couple years after you were brought here.”

“What do you mean by after I was ‘brought here,’” Trix questioned.

Jinx sat down next to her younger sister and tried to explain, “Trix, I’m a fairy and a wizard, so you are too. We are sorcerers because our true parents are. Mom and Dad aren’t our true mom and dad.”

Trix got up and went and sat on her father’s lap, “Who are our parents then?”

“Alexis and James, the famous magicians,” Zully answered.

Trix’s eyes looked like they were going to pop out of her face. She did not say a word. It was like all of a sudden she was mute, or someone had locked her mouth. Her father patted her head and hugged her tightly. “This is going to be a big and difficult change for all of us,” he whispered.

Jinx ran upstairs into her bedroom to think. She lay on her bed thinking about what had happened to her life. Trix and Zully came into Jinx's room and lay on the pink rug, also deep in thought. Jinx thought of the boliqua and wondered if there were other magical creatures. *Are there unicorns?* she thought. *Or dragons?* Jinx imagined what they might look like. Trix and Zully faded away on the rug and in their place a dragon sat in the same spot as Trix and a unicorn in the same spot as Zully.

Chapter 5
The Ride with Clouds

"What did you do?" asked the unicorn looking at Jinx.

"Sorry, Zully," Jinx said wondering how she was ever going to control her powers.

Suddenly, flames rose up from the rug until they almost reached the ceiling. Apparently, Trix, who was now a dragon, was trying to speak or perhaps she was upset.

We need water, Jinx thought. Just as she thought it, water began to pour from the ceiling putting out the flames and soaking the dragon. Jinx closed her eyes and carefully imagined Trix and Zully clearly. She was relieved when they turned back into their own selves again.

“Sorry,” Trix said looking at the soaking wet rug.

“It’s not your fault!” Jinx told her. “I’m the one that turned you into a dragon in the first place!”

“Pack your bags! Pack your bags!” a small voice said from above. Nana had heard the emergency and flown into the bedroom. “We have to get going immediately! You’ve got to take these tests as soon as possible before you do any damage that is irreversible!” She waved her wand and six bags appeared. She waved it again and the bags became full. She waved it one last time and names appeared on each bag – one for Jinx, Trix, Nana, Granny, Jack and Zully.

Jinx picked up her bag and Zully’s bag, Nana grabbed her tiny bag and Trix got her bag.

“Granny, Dad!” Jinx called.

Granny and Jack hurried into the room. When they saw their bags, they grabbed them too.

“Jinx, we need your help with this,” said Granny. “We all need to imagine rising up into a cloud and riding it. We’ll do the getting to Malunia part.”

“Got it,” said Jinx trying to sound confident. But Jinx was full of worries. *What if someone falls through the clouds? What if someone doesn't make it?*

"Three," said Granny as she put out three fingers. "Two." She dropped a finger. "One!"

The three sorcerers closed their eyes. Nana and Granny waved their wands. A door appeared on the ceiling. It slowly slid open. Jinx felt herself rise into the air like she had in the middle of the night. They all rose up, up, up out of the door and high into the sky. Jinx opened her eyes and looked down at her ordinary sized house that now looked like an ant. Jinx looked around at her family. She had no idea why Trix wanted wings because she looked like she was doing a silent scream. Her father looked pretty freaked out too. Sweat was falling from his forehead, his lips were trembling and he made sure to never look down. Jinx turned to her grandmother. Nana seemed to not trust the spell as she flapped her wings so hard it made her shoulder length straight gray hair blow. Granny was the only one who looked relaxed. She was smiling and enjoying the view.

Eventually, they were level with the clouds. They went right through one. It felt like a pile of cozy blankets. Jinx thought how nice it would be to fall asleep. Then, all of a sudden they stopped and started falling. But it was not long before they landed on the cloud.

All Jinx's worries came to her again. *What if someone falls through? What if someone doesn't make it?* she worried. She looked at everyone and started counting to make sure everyone was on the cloud. "One, two, three, four, five."

"Ahhhh!"

Jinx looked down. Something was falling quickly right below them. It was a man and Jinx immediately realized that it was her father. Jinx quickly tried to think of what to do, but she did not have any ideas.

Luckily, her grandmothers saw her father too. Granny waved her wand and wings appeared on her father's back. He furiously flapped and flapped, but it was no use. He wasn't able to fly back up to the cloud. Nana waved her wand and she grew. She grew so much that when she finished, she was bigger than a normal human. The cloud was miles above the ground, so her father was still falling. Nana dove off the cloud into the sky. She fell deeper and deeper using her wings to push herself faster. When she finally caught up to him, she grabbed Jack by the leg and pulled him up. Using her enormous and strong body, she was able to pull him back up to the cloud.

Jinx and Trix hugged him the second Nana put him on the cloud. They had almost lost their mother and father in only twenty-four hours. "Loosen your grip," Jack choked.

The cloud started moving. It zoomed like an airplane. Something tiny appeared in the distance. It got bigger and bigger and then a loud noise started coming from it. It was a familiar sound. Jinx looked back at everyone else, except no one was there. She was all alone. Someone tapped her on the shoulder. "Look down," squeaked a familiar voice. It was Nana. But Jinx still couldn't see anyone. However freaked out she was, she took the advice and looked down. Except, what she saw, scared her even more. She shrieked. She saw the cloud, but only the cloud, as her body was gone.

"It's okay," Granny's voice said behind her. "We're only invisible so that the people on the helicopter don't see us. It will fade away." This did not help Jinx. She always loved magic and she believed in magic, but she never thought it would actually reveal itself to her.

The cloud started zooming another way and eventually the helicopter was out of sight. Everyone turned visible again and Jinx asked, "Trix, Dad, how did you stay so calm?"

"I'm more used to magic than you are," Trix replied simply shrugging.

That's totally not true! thought Jinx.

"I'm guessing your grandmothers put some kind of a spell on me during out talk last night to help me get through all of this," Jack guessed winking at Nana and Granny.

Quack! Quack! Quack! A flock of ducks flew above the cloud.

"What do we do?" asked Jinx.

"Nothing. They'll ignore us. I see them all the time when I'm riding clouds and magic carpets."

"Magic carpets!" Jinx screamed happily jumping on the cloud.

"Yay!" Trix joined in.

"Girls, sit down and let's have a picnic," said Granny waving her wand.

Jinx sat down, but she was no longer sitting on the cloud. She was sitting on a red and white checkered blanket on top of the cloud. Nana waved her wand and the best picnic Jinx had ever seen appeared on the blanket. In the center, there was watermelon, with chocolate covered strawberries and cinnamon covered apples. There was also a tray of sandwiches. In the desert corner, there was an enormous cookie jar, a birthday cake for Jinx and also, Jinx's favorite, bubble gum. Before anyone could stop her, Jinx grabbed a piece of the gum.

"Lunch first," Nana said. "Spit it out."

Jinx did as she was told and spit it out into her napkin. Her napkin immediately disappeared and was replaced by a clean, new one. She put her hands back on the cloud so she could feel the warm blanket, want-to-sleep feeling. However, this time, that was not what she felt. What she felt was not a good feeling. It made a strange feeling flood through her body. The feeling when you had been enjoying a sunny day with your friends, then all of a sudden, it starts pouring. She looked back; she did not see a big, fluffy white cloud. Instead she saw a gray shrinking cloud.

"What is it, Jinx?" asked Granny.

Jinx looked beneath the cloud. She could see millions of rain drops pouring out of the cloud. "Granny, what happens it if rains?" Jinx finally asked.

"Well, the cloud then soon disappears. But, then we

fall onto the rainbow bridge," Granny answered while chewing on a cinnamon covered apple. "Why?"

"Because it's raining," replied Jinx as lightning struck level with their cloud.

"Just wait for the rainbow," Granny said taking a look at the thunderstorm herself.

Boom!

What happens when the clouds disappear? Jinx wondered still very confused. The cloud still had about one fourth left to shrink, but then it suddenly disappeared. When Jinx saw the cloud vanish beneath them, she realized that it must have happened because that was what she was thinking. It instantly stopped raining.

"Ahhhh!" screamed Jake, Trix, Jinx and Zully.

Nana was flying and Granny seemed to trust the rainbow wherever it was. Granny was right though, because in just a few moments, they all stopped on the clearest rainbow Jinx had ever seen. It felt like she was walking on air but she was not worrying about falling because the rainbow made only happy thoughts come to her and a feeling of joy.

"Get off at the next cloud you see that is close

enough for us to reach," Nana reminded the rest of them.

They walked on the rainbow for what seemed like miles. Zully finally yelled, "I see one! I see a cloud!" Zully bounded after the cloud with everyone following. She took a long jump and landed on the cloud, still followed by everyone else.

Jinx felt the same extremely cozy feeling as the last cloud, except this time, she could not control herself and she went to sleep.

Chapter 6
Malunia Lane and the Ball of Control

"Jinx! Jinx!" whispered Trix, shaking her sister awake.

Jinx opened her eyes. Trix was kneeling next to her and Zully was standing over her as she had done when Jinx had fainted. Zully gave Jinx a slobbery lick and then backed away.

"What hap –who – where are we?" Jinx questioned.

"We're at Malunia, Jinx! Come on!" Trix answered as quickly as possible.

Jinx sat up. The cloud was now very low where Jinx could just step off it onto the ground. It was in a forest and to her left were two enormous golden doors with the word "Malunia" floating in mid-air above them. Jinx tried to see what was behind the doors, but from this distance, it only looked like more trees.

"Come on," said Granny, as she and Nana went to the doors. As Granny tugged at the doors, Granny and Nana said together, "Welcome to your new home!"

Inside the doors, there was a different world. Elves, like the ones Jinx had watched take the odd woman away and go through the portal, were here, except these had hair and they scurried in and out of holes in trees carrying batches of cookies or some other meal, treat or ingredient. Fairies, like Nana, flew into other holes in trees or into tiny huts. Wizards walked into a distant castle. Bees buzzed and flew from flower to flower collecting nectar. Humming birds hummed. Butterflies with enormous, rainbow-colored wings flew all around. The flowers actually danced and sang. Everything was beautiful, everything was happy and everyone was happy.

"Come," said Nana.

Amazed, everyone walked through the golden doors. An elf carrying a bag of flour saw them all and he pointed right at Jinx and cried, "She's here! She's here!

Jinx Silverspark is here!"

Jinx saw many tiny heads, including fairies and elves poke out of holes in trees. She saw some wizards stop and stare. Two familiar wizards stepped forward. The woman looked like a grown up Jinx and the man had shaggy brown hair and hazel eyes. Jinx recognized them as famous magicians in the human world. They were Alexis and James; the ones that Jinx had recently figured out were her true parents. Each of them was crying with happiness.

Jinx looked at the only father she had ever known. Jack let a tear fall down his cheek. He was trying to be happy for his daughters, but was afraid he was going to lose them.

The small group was soon surrounded by staring sorcerers. Jinx and Trix hugged their father tightly and then slowly walked to greet their true parents. It was very awkward.

"Hello," whispered Jinx after a long moment of silence.

"Jinx," said James, remembering her as a baby, "hello."

"Hello," Alexis waved. "You've grown so much."

"And Trix," said James, as Trix joined Jinx, "hello."

"Hello," said Trix through the same kind of tears as Jack.

"Hello," said Alexis.

Not knowing how to react, Jinx looked down at the stars on her legs. Then, she realized something, James had the same silver stars that she did, but Alexis had none at all. "Alexis – mom, where are your stars?"

"Well, I'm actually a fairy. I used magic to grow and to lose my wings. That is why you are half fairy. Nana is my mother," Alexis explained. "But I got this so I could keep my fairy symbol." She turned around and showed them what looked like a giant tattoo of a fairy's wings on her back.

"Come on, Jinx, Trix, and Jack. Is that your dog? Well, she's welcome to come see your new home too," said James. "Hopefully, it won't feel quite so weird after some sleep."

They walked a long time, down a winding, beautiful path surrounded by rose bushes.

"I love Malunia!" Nana shouted happily as she did a cartwheel in the air.

"That's some grandmother you've got there," whispered Granny as she watched Nana skipping in the air.

"What is Malunia Lane?" asked Jinx curiously.

"This is Malunia Lane," Granny said, proud for living in such a beautiful place.

"I love it," said Jinx looking around.

Finally, they reached the castle that had been off in the distance.

"Welcome to your new home," said Granny.

"No!"

"Yes!"

"No!"

"Yes!"

"Yeah!" shouted Jinx and Trix. All of their worries about their mom and meeting their new parents were momentarily forgotten at the sight of the castle. They both raced inside and could not wait to explore. The castle was beautiful. When they first walked in, there was an extremely large, but empty room. The only pieces of furniture in the room were a gold and red throne and many beautiful portraits of previous most powerful sorcerers. One painting of a baby stood out to Jinx. The baby had twinkling, brown eyes even in the portrait and blonde hair that had just started to grow. It was unquestionably Jinx as a baby. Trix looked around the room, but this was not very interesting for her, so she climbed a spiraling staircase. However, Jinx stayed and admired the room. She walked down a thin red carpet that started at the entrance of the castle and ended at the end near the thrones. She slowly and carefully sat down on one of the seats. She felt almost as if she was on the cloud again. She felt as if this was where she was meant to be.

Jack, Alexis, James, Granny and Zully walked into the room and Nana flew in.

"You've found your seat," said Alexis, in awe.

Zully bounded over to Jinx and curled up in her lap. Zully was very heavy although Jinx did not care. She stroked her thick, long coat of golden fur softly. It felt weird. Although Zully's appearance was that of a dog, she did not have many dog habits so Jinx often forgot that Zully was in fact a dog.

"Would you like to see your room?" James asked.

"Sure," Jinx replied as Zully got down from her lap.

Jinx was expecting to go up the spiral staircase, but instead Granny snapped her fingers and a big glass box appeared. Alexis clapped her hands and the box opened. Jinx followed the others in and James raised his hand. With nothing pulling it, the box started to rise.

"You'll be using this until you learn how to fly," Nana explained fluttering her wings as she sat on Alexis' shoulder.

Jinx stared out the glass walls. They went up floor after floor after floor. The glass box traveled right through some of the floors.

Finally, they arrived at the top floor. It was only one huge, circular room. The ceiling was a large, huge dome and a deck was around the complete exterior of the room. Jinx opened a sliding glass door to the deck and stepped out. She could see all of Malunia.

"That's your school," Granny said pointing at a small, but beautiful building. It was surrounded with colorful flowers.

"What?" Jinx asked surprised. "My old school was bigger than that!"

"It's a lot bigger than it looks," said Alexis. "Trust me, I went to that school."

"That's the magic tool store," Nana said from Jinx's hand.

"That's the mall," said James pointing what looked like a small box. "It's also much bigger inside."

Jinx spotted a large cement building with high fences around it. It looked like several wizards were guarding it. The building did not seem to fit with the rest of the beautiful town of Malunia. "What's that?" Jinx asked pointing to it.

"That is Sorson," answered Granny.

"Sorson?" Jinx wondered.

"It's the sorcerer prison. Only the most evil sorcerers go to that prison. Once you are there, you have no chance of escaping," explained Granny.

Jinx took one last look at Sorson and then turned and Jinx walked back inside her room. She had a cloud as a bed. A large mirror hung on the walls with a golden frame resting above a table with no legs. On the table, there was a beautiful tiara that was half silver and half bronze. Jinx looked at it more closely and noticed that in the middle, there was a large gold star with smaller silver stars around it on the bronze side and on the silver side there was a pair of bronze wings. Almost like there was a magnet connecting them, Jinx picked the tiara up and put it into her hair. Her wings sank more into her back and all the stars on her legs moved while her one gold star grew.

"It's yours," said Alexis, bursting into tears again. "The last time I saw you in person, you were just a little baby and now, now you've found your tiara!"

"It's okay," James encouraged. "We'll make up for the ten years we've been separated."

That night, Jinx sat up in bed, her eyes remained closed as she was still in a wonderful dream about her future as a sorcerer. Her body rose slightly over her bed, but she was still asleep as she fell off the cloud bed. She landed on the floor with a thump. However, she was still in a deep, deep sleep and she was still happy in her dream thinking about her future.

Wazilma smiled as she stood on Jinx's balcony and peeked into the window watching the sleeping young sorcerer. Her plan was working. She gripped the human magnet tighter and as she did so, Jinx started to slide across her bedroom floor towards Wazilma with the magnet.

Creak! Creak! Creak!

"On no!" mumbled Wazilma. "Someone must have heard Jinx fall to the floor," Wazilma mumbled to herself as she scurried to the edge of the balcony. She tried to disappear, but discovered that her powers had weakened and she could no longer do that spell. Wazilma did the first thing she could think of, but it was not too smart. She dropped the magnet and jumped off the balcony. She fell so far that someone normal would have died. However, she had enough power left that she was able to survive with only two black eyes and a bloody nose. While this attempt to capture Jinx failed, Wazilma was confident that she was going to get Jinx soon. She limped off to her magic carpet.

The sun shone over Malunia early the next morning and through the thin violet curtains that draped over the sliding glass doors in Jinx's bedroom. Jinx was still lying on her fuzzy turquoise rug dreaming happily. She was at the school house with a bunch of friends. She was not hiding from bullies who teased her about believing in magic, instead she was doing the complete opposite. She was signing notebooks and she was surrounded by adoring fans. Suddenly, someone dark and evil appeared and she woke up with a fright.

At just that moment, Alexis emerged through the floor in the glass box. “Breakfast time!” she said cheerfully.

Confused as to how she ended up on the floor, Jinx got up and joined Alexis. Alexis lowered her hands and the box moved down. She looked at her daughter and said, “Hello, Jinx.”

“Hello,” said Jinx feeling nervous and awkward.

“We’ve been apart for ten years. Let’s get to know each other,” Alexis suggested.

“Um, okay. My favorite color is sky blue,” Jinx started

“Mine too! What’s your favorite thing to do?” Alexis responded.

“I like to walk through the forest.” Jinx answered

“I also love nature.” Alexis smiled at Jinx.

They went on and on finding that they were very much alike. When they reached the bottom floor, it felt like they had made up some of their time from their separated years. The entire family was already eating breakfast when Jinx and Alexis arrived. They sat next to each other and continued to see if there was anything else they could learn.

Trix shot Jinx a nasty look. She was having a harder time learning that Kate and Jack were her adopted parents. Jinx was having a difficult time too. She was worried about her mom, Kate, and was not sure what to do with all of these new parents.

Jinx watched Alexis wave her wand to make food appear on her plate. Jinx closed her eyes imagining carefully what she wanted: orange juice, pancakes and waffles with syrup. Jinx opened one eye first, scared to see what she might have done. However, the only thing wrong was that her orange juice was just an orange. Looking at the food, Jinx realized she was starving and she gobbled down her pancakes and waffles with extra syrup and swallowed the orange in big bites. When she was done, she licked her lips like a kitten that had just finished a bowl of milk.

After breakfast, Jinx set out to explore every room in the castle. There were many kitchens where maids worked hard, but happily (some even hummed and skipped) making delicious treats and meals. She found many secret closets with things like brooms, what appeared to be crystal balls, and some strange glittery powder containers labeled things like elf letters, fairy letters and wizard letters. In the bathrooms, she tried out the sinks. The water came from the air, bounced off her hand and disappeared. When Jinx finally finished exploring, she stepped back into the glass box to go back up to her room.

As she was rising, she saw a closet she had missed. She clapped her hands to open the door and jumped out as the glass box continued moving up. She landed on her feet like a cat and scurried over to the door. As she got closer, she saw glittery powder and fire. Carefully, Jinx opened the door and four faces stared at her. She opened her mouth to speak to Alexis, James, Granny and Nana but nothing came out, and instead a lot of powder came in.

"Jinx?" asked James, surprised. "What are you doing here?"

Jinx didn't answer right away as she stared around the closet. It was by far the oldest room in the castle. In every corner, there were cobwebs. A book shelf was pushed against the wall and was covered in dust. Jinx could have sworn she saw mice scurrying from corner to corner, picking up crumbs along the way. But something else caught her eye. She realized that she had not seen flames. A gold ball with large cracks and big, waving bumps was shooting around the closet.

"This is your ball of control. It helps you control your powers," Granny explained. "I put the fairy and wizard letters of J, I, N, and X powders inside the ball to make it yours."

Jinx stared at it curiously, "Well, so why is it so out of control?"

"Good question," said James. "It is a symbol of how your powers are now. As you can see, your powers are quite out of control. As soon as you grab the ball, it will turn into a perfect circle and your powers will only work when you wave your wand twice over your head."

"So, do I grab it now?" Jinx questioned.

"No! No!" Nana warned as she flew around the ball trying not to get knocked down. "It will be placed on the other side of Malunia Lane. You will have to walk from this side of Malunia to the far side of Malunia without using any magic."

"That will be easy!" Jinx interrupted.

"Jinx, your powers are out of control. It will be a bit hard. It might even take a few tries," Nana finished explaining.

Nana was right. It was harder than Jinx thought. Later that morning, Jinx walked down Malunia Lane toward her ball of control. She was staring at her toes, trying not to see anything that would distract her. Jinx tried to have her mind blank or only on getting the ball as soon as possible. No magic could happen with her focused on the ball or could it? Jinx wondered. Suddenly, Jinx broke into a run without even trying to. She ran so fast, it could not have been her. Magic had to be happening.

Uh oh, thought Jinx. *I was focused on trying to get there sooner and now I am going to get their sooner!*

The sound of breaking earth came from behind her. She tried to stop, but she could not. She had thought too much about getting there that the spell making her so fast was too strong. She forced herself to run towards the long line of rose bushes. She grabbed the thickest, strongest vine she could find and held on tightly. She could feel the magic around her fade away.

Jinx let go of the vine and turned around to see what was breaking the ground. At first, she thought it was only her imagination. But then, she saw it again. It appeared to be a giant finger probably as big as Jinx.

Crack! Crumble! More bricks broke and scattered. A second finger, even bigger than Jinx, emerged from the ground. Jinx took a step back ready to run at any moment. She did the only thing she could think of and she imagined the hand on fire. Flames rose on the giant fingers, but whatever was beneath Jinx did not seem to be scared. It touched the finger to the ground, easily putting the flame out.

Crack! Crack! Crack! Crumble! Crumble! Crack! Three more fingers broke through the bricks. Crack! Crumble! The whole hand appeared!

Jinx stepped back. Even though she did not know much about the creatures in the magical world, she knew for certain that this hand belonged to a giant. Jinx gave a tiny, terrified "Eek!" She could feel butterflies in her stomach. More bricks tumbled and the whole arm appeared. It reached forward and grabbed her foot. Then, the hand picked Jinx up and carried her all the way back to the beginning of Malunia Lane. The giant opened its hand and Jinx fell down head first. She could feel the blood rushing though her body. She was going to die! She said her last word, "Ahhh!"

"It's okay, Jinx," said James patting her on the back.

Is James in heaven too? Jinx wondered. *Is this what heaven looks like?* She opened her eyes. *Wow, it looks a lot like Malunia just upside down!*

Jinx looked up, everything was blurry. She rubbed her eyes and shook her head and looked again.

Something was sticking in her stomach. She looked down and realized it was James' shoulder. She was hanging over his shoulder.

"It's okay," said James. "Those giants only want to help. Just sometimes they don't know how." James quickly waved his wand and Malunia Lane returned to its normal state.

Jinx hopped down and stared at James waiting for him to say, "Kidding, giants are dangerous, stay away from them!" But, when that didn't happen, she decided to shake off the entire incident and focus again on capturing her ball of control.

Jinx waved at James and took off down Malunia Lane. This time, she plugged her ears and looked at her feet. She wished she could fall into a deep sleep and sleep walk all the way there. That way, she wouldn't be able to use any magic. It started off as only a doze, but then turned into a deep, deep sleep. She walked slowly and lazily up Malunia Lane. As she almost reached the ball of control, she awoke from a loud sound of tumbling bricks. She woke with a start as five fingers appeared in front of her and then the palm of the hand appeared right under Jinx. Jinx could hear big footsteps beneath her as the hand picked her up again and she landed back at the start of the lane with a big thump on the ground.

This time, without a word, James fixed the lane and Jinx started limping down Malunia Lane for the third time. She could feel it this time, she had courage. She could do this! She took off in a painful run trying to shake off the pain in her leg after being dropped twice by a giant.

She was only seconds away from the ball when she stopped. She fell backwards because the ground ahead of her had started to slant and move around as a different hand now emerged from the ground. The last hand had pale skin covered with freckles of all sizes. This hand had brown skin and was surprisingly even bigger. A scream rose from below the ground and could be heard by everyone. It filled the air and rattled the ground. Loud, echoing stomps could also be heard and the two combined together were causing an earthquake.

Jinx was frightened and ran as fast as she could toward her family. Many other sorcerers and her family members were rushing to her. Looking back at the hand, Jinx could see brave sorcerers attempting to push the hand back under the ground. However, the hand was strong and was destroying everything it could reach. Many fairies were smashed like bugs and wizards and elves just managed to escape. Sorcerers waved their wands attempting to stop the giant from hurting

Malunia and its citizens, but they only hurt each other.

Then, it occurred to her, she was the most powerful sorcerer here, why was she not helping? Jinx waved goodbye to her family as she moved closer to the giant's hand and wondered whether she would be the superhero or if she would die. Then, she would not be able to save her mom and that would allow Wazilma to become the most powerful sorcerer again.

Jinx stood close to the hand and could feel millions of eyes watching her hopefully. It was not helping as it was only putting more pressure on her. She focused all of her attention, closed her eyes and saw Malunia Lane how it was only moments ago. She pictured it beautiful, like it had been just that morning, not the ugly thing it had become. She imagined all of the fairies, elves and wizards safe. Jinx heard gasps and cries. *Oh, no! What have I done wrong?* Jinx worried. She opened her eyes. She had not done anything wrong, she was staring at what she had seen with her eyes closed and even the giant's hand was gone.

Jinx realized that the people that had gasped were smiling and the people who had cried were crying with happiness. She remembered that she still needed to get the ball. But, she could not do it now. The pale giant hand came up and carried her back to the beginning of Malunia Lane again. Luckily, she landed on her feet this time. She began to run back to the ball, but Granny grabbed her shirt and pulled her back.

"Hold on, Jinx," she said happily. "You've already succeeded. What you –"

"But, I used magic again!" Jinx interrupted.

"You were seconds away from the ball when the giant's hand blocked you. So you would have made it. Right?" Granny explained.

"Right."

"And, that giant was obviously on Wazilma's side. We've always had a very friendly relationship with all of the giants who live beneath us. They sometimes cause a bit of damage, but it's easy to fix. That one giant must have been under Wazilma's control. You risked your life to save Malunia and its villagers. That's better than being selfish and only trying to get that ball. You knew, you would fail the test, but you went out of your way to save Malunia. Go get your ball, but you have already succeeded so you don't need to worry about using magic."

Jinx ran back down Malunia Lane. She knew that she must have cast the fast running spell on herself again as she got to the ball in seconds and grabbed it. The gold ball immediately became a perfect circle and all of the cracks filled up making it as smooth and shiny as a marble. Jinx did not know whether to be proud of herself or scared knowing that Wazilma still had not given up. She just gave a weak smile and looked towards her family. "So is this it?" she asked. "Are my powers under full control now?"

"No!" all four professional sorcerers replied together.

Chapter 7
Tests and Tasks

Jinx sat on the neon green sofa that floated about two inches above her carpet, reading a personal narrative by Andrea Honeymeadow about how she had used certain powerful spells on her elf tests to defeat a group of ghosts. Jinx was hoping to find some ideas for how to rid the magical world of Wazilma and save her mom. Jinx gave a startled jump as the glass box unexpectedly slid right through the floor carrying Alexis and James, her grandmothers and even Zully.

"Hello," Jinx whispered as she put down her book on the floating coffee table in front of her.

"I see you're reading Elf Tests of Unexpectedness,"

Granny said suspiciously and mysteriously examining the wide and tall book.

"Great," said James in the same suspicious and mysterious tone. "It goes perfectly well with what we will be warning you about today."

Jinx scooched back on the sofa uncomfortably.

"Read this," Alexis demanded. "Sections two and three." She dropped a heavy book on Jinx's curled up lap and that was the last anyone said. They all left immediately in the glass box without even saying good-bye.

"What's the matter with them?" Jinx wondered aloud flipping through the huge book. It was a very old book with no title or author on the front cover.

Jinx opened it and glanced at section one in the book. It was titled: The Ball of Control. Jinx had already retrieved her ball of control, so she turned to section two, which she had been told to read. She started to read:

Five Tests and Three Tasks

All sorcerers have to take tests or tasks so that their ball of control works permanently. Elves take two tests of the unexpected. Fairies take three tests of kindness. Wizards have to take three tests of danger.

Danger? Danger? Seriously! Jinx thought frustrated. *More danger! I'll never survive!* She turned back to section two.

Fairy Tests of Kindness

All Fairies must take three Tests of Kindness. Fairies are by far the smallest type of sorcerer so when they go to the human world they will have to change their appearance a bit. All three tests can take place in the human world or in Malunia. However, the human world has always worked better. If you select the human world, you must be in disguise.

The first test a fairy must take is the Test of Poverty. In the Test of Poverty, fairies have to find a poor family they can help.

The second Test of Kindness is the Test of Hurt. Fairies must find someone badly injured and help them either by curing their injury or helping them learn to have fun. (Suggestions: tell a joke, play a game)

The third task is the easiest. It is the Test of the Lonely. Fairies will find someone and make friends with them. They can also introduce him or her to other friends of theirs.

Keep in mind that in the three Tests of Kindness, magic is only used for disguises and transportation. An older sorcerer relative may help with transportation. Map Port is suggested.

Jinx finished reading with a couple of questions. "How do I disguise myself?" she wondered aloud like someone was in the room with her. "And what is Map Port?"

All of a sudden, a heavy weight lifted off her lap. The book was floating in midair with pages ripping and curling and turning the same shade of red as the cover until it was no longer a book, but instead a huge pair of red lips hanging in the air in front of Jinx.

"Hello, Jinx," said the lips. "I am Everything Every Sorcerer Needs to Know About Every Power Controlling Test or Task. But, you can call me Everything for short. I am your book."

"Um, okay, Everything," Jinx whispered trying not to sound as scared as she felt. She scooched back into the sofa again.

"So, you had some questions," Everything said.

The words inside her trying to get out escaped, "What are you?" Jinx scooched back into her sofa as far as possible. She felt like she had said something wrong.

Jinx was sure that if Everything had eyes and feet she

would be looking at her toes nervously. “I told you. Your book’s lips. I am book lips.” Everything sounded a bit offended. Jinx backed away from the lips even further causing her to tumble off the back of the sofa.

“So your questions,” said Everything, ignoring Jinx’s fall. “Well, you had questions about disguises. Isn’t it obvious? Use magic!” Everything said and if she had shoulders, she probably would shrug.

“But, what kind of magic?” Jinx questioned scooching back to a normal place on the sofa.

“Your family can help you with that,” Everything answered simply. “So, now, moving on. Your other question was about Map Port. Map Port is a sorcerer’s way to travel. First, you shout the words, ‘Mapoleodoo!’ Then, you tap the map twice with a wand where you want to go and jump into the map. Then, you’ll be there. Simple, right? That’s it. Bye!”

Bang! The thick, heavy maroon book titled Everything Every Sorcerer Needs to Know About Every Power Controlling Test or Task landed on the floating coffee table.

Jinx picked up the book again cautiously. She flipped it open to section three.

Wizard Tasks of Danger

Wizards take Tests of Danger to control their powers. This is because wizards are the biggest of the three kinds of sorcerers so they have to learn how to protect themselves and others. Elves and Fairies could not handle some of these things.

Jinx gulped and read on.

The first task is to make it through the abandoned castle on Ickrealery Island. This may seem easy because it is "abandoned," but really it is only abandoned from "living" humans. Ickrealery Island and the abandoned castle is home to many creatures, including a few naughty goblins (who guard the night blue doors), a couple ghosts (who guard the treasure you are searching for), many giants (who roam the castle day and night), and one overgrown boliqua (your treasure). This means that goblins guard the entrance, giants try to kill you as they walk around the castle and ghosts guard the boliqua. Your task is to collect one needle from around the boliqua's face and make it out of the castle.

"Oh no," whispered Jinx looking up from the book.

The second task is at a haunted house. The haunted house is home to many horrible creatures such as eight ghosts, three monsters and two elephant sized spiders. There are cobwebs everywhere. Your task is to collect one coin on the top of the wooden stairs.

"Giant s-spiders," Jinx stuttered scooching into the sofa and away from a tiny spider that was crawling on her table. *If I can't handle this spider, how will I ever survive?*

The third task is the easiest and least dangerous. Wizards will appear inside a pitch-black room and won't know where they are. They won't know what is in the room with them. They will be locked inside. Then it's up to them: which spell will they choose?

Unlike Elf and Fairy tests, you CAN use magic. And, like the Elf tests, ALWAYS BE READY FOR ANYTHING!

If you are a Wizard about to take the tasks, good luck and do not worry.

"How can I not worry?" Jinx moaned.

"I don't know," Everything said flipping back into lips.

Jinx jumped. "Don't do that, Everything! I wasn't even asking you anyway!"

"Sorry, I don't choose when I get turned into lips! Whenever someone asks a question around me, I just turn into lips!" Everything said defensively. "Who were you talking to anyways? I mean, I don't have eyes but I don't hear anyone but you."

"No one's here. I was just asking myself," said Jinx.

"Oh," Everything sighed. She turned back into the book.

Suddenly, green sparkling letters slid under Jinx's bedroom door and popped up in front of her face spelling out a message. Jinx read: GET READY! THE TESTS AND TASKS ARE TOMORROW! BE DOWN IN 30 MINUTES SO YOU CAN GET YOUR WAND!

"Huh?" Jinx wondered. "The tests and tasks are tomorrow! My wand!" Jinx decided to use her thirty minutes to go to the library hoping to find some ideas on ways to help her pass the tests.

She used the glass box to travel the two floors down to the library she had seen when she was exploring. "Open," she said quickly to the library door.

"Correct," mumbled the door lazily as the door opened up.

"That's still your password?" shouted the other side of the door from her place facing the inside of the library. "You're so boring, Titchy!"

Jinx ran inside the multi-colored library as Titchy closed slowly and lazily behind her.

"Hey, Jinx," said the inside of the door, obviously trying to sound cool.

Jinx had no idea why both the inside and outside of the library door could speak and also how the door had known her name, but she just replied, "Hey, umm."

"Paisley," the door finished for Jinx. "My name is

Paisley."

"Right," Jinx sighed, continuing to walk into the library. She didn't have time to have a long conversation with a door so she moved quickly.

Jinx remembered many nooks and corners from when she had explored but not all of it. You could spend a year wandering around the library and still find new fun reading spots and tiny sections. Maybe it was because it changed with magic, or maybe it was just so massive there would always be a new place. Jinx glanced at an empty desk hoping to find a librarian, but there was no one there. She knocked softly on the white with purple, pink and blue polka dotted desk hoping to get someone's attention.

Suddenly, a miniature librarian jumped off an orange chair and landed onto the desk. She couldn't have been more than a couple of inches tall. "Hello there," squeaked the tiny librarian happily. "My job is – wait, are you – no it couldn't be her – although she did just move here. Yippy!" She jumped into the air and fell off the desk just barely grabbing on to the edge of it before falling. "It's really, really, really, nice to meet you," she squeaked as the one hand hanging onto the desk started slipping.

“Here,” said Jinx scooping her up into her hands and setting her back on the desk. The whole time the little librarian stared up at her, eyes open and mouth in a huge smile.

“Hi Jinx, I see you’ve met my little helper,” said a kind voice from behind Jinx.

Jinx turned around and saw a normal size version of the miniature sized little librarian standing in front of her. She was a wizard with twinkling hazel eyes behind her enormous green glasses. She had brown wavy hair that went to her shoulders with natural blue highlights. “I was just helping someone,”

“Who?” Jinx asked immediately, curious as she had run into very few people in the castle.

An elf stepped out from behind the librarian. Jinx recognized this elf immediately. Freckles covered the elf’s pale skin and her messy red hair was in braids that looped up and were tied with light blue bows. The elf was wearing a checkered dress with matching blue ribbons. The elf immediately recognized Jinx too with her blonde hair that could easily be mistaken for white and her brown eyes that shimmered beautifully.

Chapter 8
Lola and Magical Tools

"Hi, I'm Sprinkles Silverswirl," the librarian said politely to Jinx. She noticed the two girls staring at each other. "Jinx, this is Lola Goldenstream and Lola this is Jinx Silverspark," she told them.

"I missed you!" they both shouted at the same time ignoring the librarian.

"Shhh! It's a library!" Sprinkles reminded them.

Lola and Jinx hugged each other tightly. Even with Jinx on her knees, she was still taller than Lola.

"You're an elf?" asked Jinx.

"Yeah," said Lola gloomily. But then she yelled happily, "You're the most powerful sorcerer in the world!"

"We definitely have a lot of catching up to do! But right now, I need help looking for some good books. Want to help me?" asked Jinx hopefully.

"Of course," Lola said. So they set off into the never ending library pulling out books of all colors and sizes.

"Remember, I need something about how to get past goblins, ghosts and giants," Jinx told Lola as she flipped through another book and added it to the growing pile at her feet.

"I give up," moaned Lola.

"We have to keep trying!" Jinx encouraged her. "There has to be something useful in here somewhere."

Just as she said that a loud coughing noise came from outside the main door of the library.

"Titchy!" cried Sprinkles who was standing behind her desk. "Remember, this is a library!" As Sprinkles was talking to Titchy, sparkling green letters came flooding out of Paisley's large mouth.

"Yuck!" screamed Paisley, while Titchy chuckled from the other side. "Oh, shut up, Titchy!" Paisley yelled at her.

The letters rose into the air and read: WAND.

"Oh my gosh! I forgot all about my wand!" said Jinx. "Bye Lola! I've got to go. I'll be back soon!"

"I want to go with you," Lola cried, after picking up her own green wand and running as fast as her tiny legs could carry her to catch up to Jinx who was already quickly heading to the library door. "We do everything together! Remember?"

"I didn't forget," Jinx said to Lola approaching Paisley and pulling on the doorknob. The door didn't open. Jinx tried again and then Lola tugged on the door too. But, still Paisley didn't budge.

"Open up!" demanded Jinx.

"No," Paisley refused. "Give me the exit password."

"There's no such thing as an exit password!" Lola complained.

"Things change," said Paisley simply.

"I'm in a hurry, open up!" Jinx yelled.

"No!" Paisley refused. "You didn't have time to talk with me before. I guess I'm just an unimportant door.

Well, now I don't feel like helping you!"

"Just open up, Paisley, please," said Sprinkles, setting the book she was looking at down and walking over to the door.

"No," Paisley repeated.

"I'm sorry, Paisley," Jinx apologized. "I'm just in a bit of a rush today and kind of distracted."

"Well, you don't seem to be in a rush with the little elf girl!" Paisley responded, still not opening the door.

"Titchy! Open up! Some girls want to leave and Paisley won't open," Sprinkles called to the other side of the door.

"Zzzzzz," was the only answer they received from Titchy.

"Useless," Sprinkles sighed shaking her head.

Jinx and Lola had lost their patience and they started banging on the door. No one came to help them and Paisley continued to refuse to let them out.

Finally, Sprinkles announced, "I think I have an idea."

"What?" questioned Jinx.

"There's a trap door somewhere around here. I saw

it one day," explained Sprinkles. "I don't think I ever went through it, but it's worth a try. I heard it takes you down in the basement and then you can come back up into a different part of the castle."

Jinx glanced down at Lola who had the same nervous expression as Jinx. However, they both could not go anywhere, so what choice did they have? They followed Sprinkles to new sections of the library and through narrow hallways. Wherever they looked, books still lined the shelves. Finally, they went through a dark narrow hall. This one was different, as not a single book was in sight. With each step, it got darker and darker.

"Ouch!" Jinx screeched. "I think I just walked into a door!"

"Good," Sprinkles sounded relieved. "We're going the right way."

"Where are we?" wondered Lola.

No one answered.

Sprinkles pulled out her wand. She felt around in the dark and then stuck it in the key hole and surprisingly it clicked and turned. Jinx yanked the heavy door open. The light from the room ahead let Jinx see that the door was small, a half circle, and wooden. She bent down through the door holding Lola's hand. Lola could stand on her tip toes and she still would not even be close to the extremely low ceiling, and Sprinkles, who had to duck, trailed behind them.

The room had bookshelves all over the place and was covered in a beautiful flower patterned wallpaper. Sprinkles headed right toward the middle of the room. She crossed her fingers and got on her knees. She looked under the nearest bookshelf. Meanwhile, Lola and Jinx stared through the skinny path between bookshelves, very confused. Sprinkles looked up with a grin on her face. Without a word, she started pushing the bookshelf. When Jinx saw that the shelf had not moved an inch, she stepped forward to help her. They finally pushed the shelf out of the way and Jinx could see three thick, rusty silver bars blocking a small, long hole. Sprinkles pushed it open with all her might. They looked down into the hole, but it was very dark and they could not see to the bottom.

"Well, hopefully this isn't bye forever," whispered Sprinkles just before she lowered herself into the deep hole. Jinx and Lola listened to hear the thump on the ground of Sprinkles landing, but they only heard the loud, echoing screams of Sprinkles that soon died away.

"Let's go together," Jinx decided finally.

"I don't think so! I'm afraid of heights!" I'd rather be stuck in this library forever," Lola complained.

Jinx sighed, "Well, we've handled bullies before together. This is bigger, but I think we can do it! Come on!" She doubted she had encouraged Lola, since she hardly believed herself. She nervously took a seat on the edge of the hole with her legs dangling down the inside. Lola carefully put her hands on Jinx's shoulders.

Jinx scooched forward. Then, they were off and their screams and shouts now echoed throughout. Jinx soon realized that they were sliding down a tunnel. They were moving so fast that they hardly realized when they shot right through a portal. The portal felt strange, almost like cake batter.

"Whoa!" screeched Lola as they each landed on their backs on a hard floor after they shot out of the other end of the portal.

Sprinkles stood near them. "I guess this is the basement of the castle," she sighed. Jinx glanced around the basement seeing nothing except dust and cobwebs. "So," said Sprinkles loudly pointing to two very tall staircases. "One of these goes up to the first floor of the castle ...the other, well I don't know. It could possibly be the room that I've heard holds dangerous animals. I've heard about it, but I've never seen it. "

"Sprinkles, you go that way and we'll go up that one," decided Jinx.

"Got it," Sprinkles replied hurrying up the staircase on the right.

Jinx looked at Lola, then at the left staircase and then back at Lola. "Ready?" she said.

"I'll never be ready, but let's get it over with," whispered Lola.

"Come on," said Jinx trying to be brave. "There's a fifty percent chance this leads to the first floor."

"Or one hundred percent chance it takes us to somewhere I don't want to be," mumbled Lola taking her first step up the creaky steps.

"Think good thoughts," Jinx suggested. "Maybe it's one hundred percent first floor. I mean, what other place would this lead to?

"I can't believe we lost a fight to a door!" mumbled Lola. "We should have just kept fighting with that door, instead of going along with Sprinkles plan."

Jinx ignored her. Soon they approached a door at the top of the stairs. They looked at each other sharing the same expression. They were both pale; Lola was even paler than usual. They could hear their teeth chattering because they were so scared and goosebumps spread around their bodies. Jinx slowly reached out her goosebump-covered arm. She grasped the rusty knob, twisted it and yanked the door open. Without even peeking inside, she immediately took steps back. Lola, also without looking inside, accidentally tumbled down several steps before catching a white pole that held up the old railing.

After Lola carefully crawled back up the stairs, together they peeked inside. Inside was a nightmare! Sprinkles had been right. A creature neither of them had ever seen before was standing in front of them. It looked like a lion, only three times as big and it had about ten extra legs and big, dangerous, long, moose antlers.

"I found it!" they heard a distance voice calling.

"That's Sprinkles!" yelled Jinx.

"I wish she had said that before we opened the door!" shrieked Lola kicking the door closed with her tiny feet.

They tumbled downstairs quickly going one hundred times faster than they had when going up. When they got to the bottom, hearts beating, and faces red and sweaty, they scurried up the other staircase and with the tiny bit of energy that they had left, they opened the door to the first floor and collapsed on the ground.

"You are so late!" grumbled Granny. "And who is this?" she asked looking at the little elf.

"Lola," replied Jinx brushing sweat off her face. She looked around and noticed all of her family members happened to be standing at the top of the stairs.

"What were you doing?" cried Alexis paying no attention to Lola. "We've been so worried! We couldn't figure out where you had gone!"

"Well, it's a long story," Jinx began.

"Good thing it's a long walk to the magic tool store. Talk and walk," Alexis demanded. Jinx and Lola did not stop talking until they got to the store.

"Interesting," said James. "I'd heard about that door before. I never knew if it was real or not. However, next time, keep fighting Paisley!"

By now they were in the magic tool store. "This is nice," said Jinx twirling a pink wand in her hand.

"That is nice," said Lola looking over Jinx's shoulder.

"Uh, oh," Jack whispered.

"What do you mean?" questioned Jinx.

"I know a lot of stuff about this world now. So, I learned that you can't just pick any wand you want even if you think it's pretty. This is the wand that is assigned to you," explained Jack holding up a long thick golden wand.

"It's not the prettiest. But, it has to be thick to hold all of your powers," explained Granny.

"I think it's beautiful!" whispered Jinx. She put the pink wand down and gently held the golden wand. She slow twirled it around in her hand.

"Can I see it?" asked Nana.

"I agree with Jinx," said Zully. "It is beautiful!"

Alexis walked over to the elf who owned the store. She was opening her bag as she was going to pay for the wand.

"Free," said the elf smiling, showing his yellow crooked and missing teeth.

"No, no!" Alexis refused. "That wand is precious! I have to pay you something!"

“No, pay me nothing,” said the elf. He shook his head and his inch-long, white mustache swayed. “She is Jinx. She is going to save us from Wazilma. The wand is free.”

Jinx overheard him and some of her excitement about the wand immediately vanished as she remembered that she still needed to defeat Wazilma and save her mom. Alexis kindly thanked the elf and the entire group walked out of the store.

Jinx gripped her wand tightly and a rush of magic spread through her body. As soon as the door to the store closed behind her, the wand leapt out of her hand and started dancing or at least it appeared to dance as much as something can when it has no arms and legs. Fireworks shot through the tip of it as if it was celebrating the fourth of July.

“It’s celebrating that it found you,” said Lola watching the wand jump back into Jinx’s hands. “Mine did that, too.”

“What are you waiting for? Do something with it!” demanded Trix.

“Well I really want some…” began Jinx. She pictured what she wanted as she had seen her grandmothers do.

Pop! A bubble popped.

Trix crossed her arms. “I want some too!” she complained.

“Me too!” begged Lola as she watched Jinx blow another bubble. So, Jinx waved her wand again and immediately everyone was chewing bubble gum.

Chapter 9
The First Test

The next morning, Jinx stood in the massive living room in her castle. She looked down at the map below her.

"Your first Test of Kindness is the Test of Poverty," Alexis reminded Jinx. "Are you ready?"

"Yeah," Jinx lied. What if she failed the first test? She would let everyone down, especially her mother who was still trapped with Wazilma. Her heart thumped harder at the thought.

"Mapoleodoo!" said James loudly.

"That's what you say to a map to make Map Port available," whispered Nana practically sitting on Jinx's ear.

“Show us poverty near Malunia!” Alexis demanded.

A ghost-like house rose from the map, so small Nana would not be able to fit in it. The house appeared on the map right outside of Malunia. But then, Jinx looked at it more closely and realized it was not a house, but a tree house.

“Now, Jinx, it’s your turn. Tap the tree house twice with your wand, jump into the map and we’ll send you a letter of what to do next. Go!” Granny insisted. “Bye!”

Jinx looked nervously around the room at all the members of her family including Lola and Zully. Slowly, she bent down over the map and tapped the fading tree house twice with her wand. However, she was leaning awkwardly over the map and she lost her balance and tumbled into it. She quickly grabbed part of the map as her body disappeared.

“Ow, ow, ow!” Jinx screeched as she tumbled around on leafless branches. She stopped, stuck on a branch. Jinx looked around and realized that she was outside Malunia. It was winter again so there were no leaves on the trees and snow covered every inch of the ground. Unlike where Jinx had lived for almost ten years, where you could barely see your way through the trees, the tree Jinx had fallen into was the only tree for miles. She was surprised to see that she was wearing a thick winter coat. As she looked around, there was suddenly a blinding light causing her to squint. She slowly opened her eyes and saw a white envelope where the light was coming from. She quickly grabbed it and the light died down the same way her last glowing letter had done. She ripped open the envelope messily and read a scribbled letter:

Dear Jinx,

Now that you are at the right place, your job is to help the people in the tree house. You probably will need to come back to the castle and collect some items.

After you've met the family so you can better see how to help them, use the map and say, "Mapoleodoo!" Then say, "Show me Silverspark's castle!" The castle should appear. Tap twice on the castle and jump in.

Good luck!

Love,

All the Silversparks, Nana, Lola, Dad (Jack), and Zully

The map? Where was the map? Jinx looked around and soon saw a corner of the map peeking out from behind a pile of snow on a branch above her. She reached up and gently pulled the map down, however it caught on a sharp, thin branch and the map tore in half right down the middle!

Oh no! thought Jinx. *The map!*

A small sparkle blew out of her wand almost as if it was reminding her of her power. Just as she was about to use the wand to repair Map Port, Jinx remembered something else, *I can't use magic right now!* Hoping that the map would still work she stuffed both pieces of it into a small pocket in her coat. Slowly and carefully, holding onto a thick, trustworthy branch, Jinx got up.

Now that she was standing, she could see a small, dusty tree house above her. She climbed to the top of the tree where the tree house was. Thankful for her many hours spent on the monkey bars in school, Jinx was easily able to make it to the top.

When she reached the top of the treehouse, she peeked inside a carved, open, round window. There was no dust-free spot. It smelled horrible like rotten eggs.

The wood was cracked in many places, and it looked like it was full of splinters ready to shoot right into someone's foot. A thin ladder hung from the tree house floor near a carved, open door. It swayed a bit as a skinny and dirty boy wearing only rags climbed up it. Sweat spilled out from under his shaggy, messy hair. He was holding a large blue bucket full of water.

"Got the water, mama!" he said as he reached the top, obviously very proud of himself.

Jinx looked in the tree house again. Four other people, also wearing rags, worked very hard. The youngest one scrubbed the wood floor with rags and muddy water. Another young girl, probably about Jinx's age, washed herself with a neon green leaf that was probably the brightest thing in the house besides her mother's beautiful, blue, sparkling eyes. The mother sat on her knees cleaning extra clothing with the muddy water her son had brought her, probably from a rain puddle.

On the land a little beyond the treehouse, Jinx could see a boy, probably about fifteen and most likely in the same family because of the shaggy, strawberry blonde hair. He was picking what looked like edible plants and putting them in a handmade basket as he walked towards the bottom of the tree.

Jinx did not know what to say or do, so she just said, "Hello," as she peeked through the window.

"Eek!" everyone in the tree house jumped. All the water spilled, the leaf fell to the ground and the extra rags lay on the ground in the spilled water.

"Hello," Jinx repeated.

"Who are you?" asked the mother cautiously, motioning her children to her.

"Jinx. Jinx Silverspark," replied Jinx, gripping her branch tighter.

"That's an odd name. Jinx. What are you doing here?" questioned the teenage boy climbing into the tree house, the basket swinging on his arm.

"I just want to help," muttered Jinx shrugging. Now that she was here, she realized that she hadn't fully thought this through.

"We don't want your help!" the youngest girl spat.

Jinx climbed through the small, open window as the family backed up even further.

"Listen, Jinx. Our father died at a young age, leaving us with no money. It's none of your business, so GET

OUT!" the teenage boy screamed.

Jinx ignored him. "Don't you ever want a real place to live?" Jinx gently patted the old wall of the tree house. "Real food to eat?" She gestured to the basket the boy was holding. "Nice, comfortable clothes to wear?" She picked up a dirt-covered extra rag.

When she looked back at the family, they each seemed to be day dreaming, staring into space with smiles on their faces.

"That would be nice," said the older girl still half in a doze.

"I agree," murmured the younger girl.

"Fine," sighed the mother, looking around her house. "We'll give you a chance. What can you do to help us though?"

"Yes!" Jinx murmured through a fist pump. "I'm not sure yet," she said to the mother. "But, I'll be back as soon as I can!" This was one step closer to becoming a trained sorcerer and becoming a trained sorcerer was one step closer to rescuing her mom.

Jinx climbed out the window, her thick coat scratching on the old wood. She climbed down the tree so that the family would not see her as she pulled out the map, hoping it would work in two pieces. But, when she unfolded it, it was in just one piece. There was not even a crease from being scrunched up in her pocket. Not knowing how to react, she shrugged.

"Mapoleodoo! Show me Silverspark's Castle," she whispered, so the family would not see her. Quite a few castles appeared on the map. One was pink and purple, while another looked like an evil castle. There was a bronze palace and even a green with blue polka dots castle. But the other one, Jinx was sure, was hers. The gold with radiant white stars told her that it was definitely the Silverspark's Castle. Plus, it was a little bit bigger than the other castles. Her wand shimmered as she tapped the beautiful castle.

"Three, two..." she whispered to herself. "One!" Jinx dove into the map.

Only seconds later, she fell with a loud thump onto the hard wood floor of the living room. It was awfully hot to be wearing such a thick coat, so while staring back at her family staring at her, she struggled to take off the massive coat. Immediately, her wings that had been tucked under the coat popped together.

"So, how'd it go?" asked Lola.

“I’ve got a plan,” was all Jinx said. She left her family in the living room and started gathering materials from around the castle.

Jinx used some glue she had found deep in her suitcase to tape a sign to a small basket she had found in a closet. The sign said:

Please Donate! A family outside Malunia is stuck living in a tree house. They need all the help they can get! Thank you!

Jinx Silverspark

Jinx placed the sign with the basket outside the castle hoping to attract attention from Malunia’s citizens. Right away, a fairy flew over to the basket and dropped some money into the basket. Jinx glanced at the money. She recognized the person on the money. However, it was definitely not a president. Instead it was herself, Jinx Silverspark.

“What?” Jinx stuttered. The fairy stopped midair and turned around. She was level with Jinx’s eyes.

“Oh my!” the fairy gasped. “That sign says Jinx Silverspark! You’re Jinx Silverspark!”

“Yeah,” said Jinx slowly and slightly confused. “Do you know how my picture got on that money?”

“That money...” the fairy pointed at the blue money in the basket, “is called five Silversparks.”

“That’s my family’s last name,” Jinx stuttered.

“Because in Malunia, our money’s name always changes to the most powerful sorcerer’s surname,” the fairy explained.

“Sure,” said Jinx nodding slowly. The fairy tucked her purple hair behind her ear and smiled like she was looking at a celebrity. She fluttered her wings and took off out of sight.

For the next hour, Jinx stood by the basket thanking elves, fairies and wizards who were willing to help by adding Silversparks to the basket. Then, an elf strolled by as if she owned the place. She eyed Jinx suspiciously, narrowing her eyes until her evil purple eyes could barely be seen. Jinx watched the elf as she walked slowly by, reading the sign.

When the elf finished, she stopped, pulled down a pair of dark sunglasses and her face got even nastier, if possible. She smiled a smile that gave Jinx the feeling that this girl was not someone to be friends with.

“Who are you?” asked Jinx to the elf, who was now circling Jinx and looking her up and down.

"Shanna," said the elf slowly. "Shanna Beautywhirl." The elf continued to walk in circles around the basket staring at the basket and at Jinx.

"What are you doing?" Jinx asked.

The elf ignored her. Instead, she took out a wand. She waved the wand and a large piece of paper shot out of the end of the wand. Shanna used her wand to write a note onto the piece of paper. She wrote:

Don't donate! Jinx Silverspark only wants to use the money for herself! She's a liar! DON'T DONATE!

Then, she magically hung the sign next to Jinx's on the basket with a piece of red tape that sprang from her wand.

"Ugh!" cried Jinx. She tore the paper off the basket and crumpled it up, scowling at Shanna. The elf watched and smiled as an identical sign appeared right in the place that Jinx had just snatched it from. Jinx immediately tore that one down too. But just as quickly, it was replaced. Shanna was laughing out loud now. Jinx tried to remove it a few more times, but the mean elf's sign continued to reappear and Shanna continued to laugh louder and harder. Finally, Jinx grabbed the basket of money and stormed into the castle.

After Jinx calmed down a bit, she went to the mall outside of Malunia with Lola and Lola's mother to try to purchase items for the family in the tree house.

"We just moved from all of this normal stuff! Why are we back here?" complained Lola's mother after trying to talk to a fly that continued to land on her soft, pink scarf. "I wonder why we ever moved here!"

Jinx suddenly had millions of questions for Lola that were bubbling inside her looking for a way to escape. There just had not seemed like a good time to ask them. Finally, the questions came exploding out of Jinx's mouth, "How come you were my friend in the non-magical world when you are an elf? Why weren't you living in Malunia the whole time? Did you know you were an elf? Have you taken the Tests of Unexpected? Why were you both so tall before? Why were you in the library?" Jinx abruptly stopped talking and looked from Lola to her mom.

"Um, well, I don't know," Lola's mom, Nylora stuttered looking at her shoes. She did not bother to look Jinx in the eye.

"Some secret she has about my dad and brothers," Lola murmured and shrugged.

"What was that Lola?" Nylora snapped, looking with piercing eyes at her daughter.

"Nothing," Lola lied immediately. Lola looked at Jinx and sadly shook her head. Jinx figured she was not going to get any answers now either.

The more the three walked, the more attention they attracted. Although Jinx's wings were not visible under her layers of clothing, she had two elves trailing behind her.

"Oh, this looks like a nice store," Nylora said, grabbing Lola by the shoulders and steering her into a dark store and motioning Jinx to follow.

"Let's go somewhere else," suggested Jinx. "The family in the treehouse already has enough dark things. We need to put some color into their lives!"

She jingled all of the money in her pocket and then remembered that they were all Silversparks. She could not spend the money here.

"Lola, what about my money?" wondered Jinx. "It's all Silversparks."

"I'll help you with that," said Lola steering Jinx to a corner.

"No! I can do it!" offered Nylora.

"Mom," said Lola. "I can do this."

Nylora murmured something like "Wama'll be 'ad at me! Maybe 'ven 'ill me!"

Lola rolled her eyes before waving her wand to change all of the pictures of Jinx on the money to Presidents.

"You're right Jinx. Let's go somewhere else," Lola agreed.

So, Jinx and Lola skipped off out of the store. "You can wait here, Mom!" Lola called as the door swung closed behind them and the little bell gave a jingle.

"Fine! Fine, I'll just stay here and wait! Left out of the fun, only me and Map Port!" Nylora hissed attracting even more attention. "What are you looking at monkey-heads?" Nylora bellowed at all of the people who were staring at the small woman.

"I swear, sometimes my mother drives me crazy. I wish I could take a long break from her," Lola complained to Jinx.

Jinx didn't respond. She didn't know what she would do if she had a mother like that. Thinking about mothers, made her think about Kate and worry and hope that she was okay.

"That looks like a nice store," suggested Lola pointing to a colorful store with pants folded nicely on shelves and shirts and dresses hanging neatly on display.

"Perfect," whispered Jinx, as she walked into the store trying to focus on the task rather than worry about her mom right now.

Lola examined a pair of heavy pants while Jinx admired a sundress. Then she found a small corner of the store that had everything she needed. There were sundresses that would fit all of the girls perfectly and t-shirts and shorts for the boys and shoes for everyone.

Lola came bouncing over. "I found a great winter section," she said. "Wow! That's a great summer section." She glanced at the corner before taking Jinx's arms and dragging her away to another corner of the store. That corner of the store had thick winter coats, fluffy boots and snow suits and they were in all sizes.

After about ten minutes, Jinx was walking through the mall back to the black store with a full shopping bag swinging at her side. On her other side, Lola was walking with another full shopping bag swinging by her side.

"Well," said Jinx to Lola as they walked, "now they'll have enough clothes, but I still haven't helped them find a more comfortable place to live or be able to afford enough food. I used up all of the money I raised yesterday. How am I going to ..." Suddenly, Jinx stopped talking and walking. She was standing directly facing a bulletin board. But it was not the bulletin board that had caught her attention. It was the two signs on the bulletin board.

"This is it!" Jinx said excitedly to Lola. She began to read the first sign that was pink with a little cartoon cupcake in the corner. It said:

Love Cupcakes Bakery

Needs new employees

working from 9:00 am until 5:00 pm

Monday through Thursday

If you are a baker call 812-695-1112

Pay is $22 per hour

Thank you!

"What?" Lola asked glancing at the sign. "You want to work in a bakery?"

"Wait, Lola," Jinx murmured as she read the other sign. It was lime green and said:

SCREAM FOR ICE CREAM

Hi, we are looking for employees to work from 8:00 am until 9:00 pm from Friday to Sunday. Pay is $22 per hour. If you like making sundaes, this is your place. Call 631-528-3223

"Jinx! Hurry up!" Lola moaned wrapping her small, cold hands around Jinx's arm and attempting to pull her. However, Lola was not strong enough and Jinx stayed where she was.

"I'm coming. I'm coming," Jinx answered. But, she did not start moving until she had snapped a photo of each sign with her emergency phone.

After meeting back up with Nylora, the next stop was returning to the dusty tree house. Lola and Jinx climbed to the top of the tree as they did not trust the ladder. Nylora had refused to climb up with them but was down at the bottom, shaking branches purposely. Finally, they reached the top and climbed into the window.

Inside the tree house, everyone was doing basically the same thing Jinx had left them doing. The mother looked up and screamed in surprise, making the others jump. "Oh sorry, I wasn't expecting you," she apologized.

"That's okay," Jinx sighed. "This is my friend, Lola."

"Hi, Lola and Jinx," said the mother. "I'm – Jinx did I ever even introduce myself to you?"

"No."

"I'm Melissa. This is –" the mother said gesturing to the youngest girl.

"Emily," squeaked the youngest in a voice that sounded even younger than she looked.

"Lizzy," replied the daughter who looked about Jinx's age, giving a wave and a fake smile.

"Peter, hi," said the older boy putting his hand up to wave and starting to form a smile with his lips, but then quickly stopping himself.

"Bobby! B-O-B-B-Y!" screamed the youngest boy who was also definitely the loudest. "Got it? Not just Bob! BOB–eee!" He screeched, making an extremely high pitched noise when he said, "eee".

"Got it," Jinx said giving him a thumbs up.

Just then Jinx and Lola heard Nylora from the bottom of the treehouse screaming at them to hurry up.

"Well, I'm sorry. I guess I'll have to do this quickly,"

Jinx said. "Lola and I wanted to help you so we picked up some new clothes for you at the mall."

Melissa looked at the huge bags that both girls set down. "Thank you so much Jinx and Lola. You've been a lot of help. Thank you."

"Thank you," the children said.

"Thank you! Thank you! Thank you! T-H-A-N-C-Y-U!" screamed Bobby.

The girls heard Nylora scream impatiently again. "I'll go try to calm my mom down. Bye! Nice meeting all of you," Lola said as she climbed out the window.

Jinx stayed behind and handed the phone with the pictures of the jobs to Melissa. "There are two pictures on this phone of two signs that give you everything you need to know about getting a job at two different places. Just call the numbers if you are interested."

"Thanks," Melissa said taking the phone.

Jinx waved good bye and climbed out the window. At the bottom of the tree, Lola and Nylora continued to argue with one another.

"Let's get going," Jinx said. "It's getting late and I need to get ready for my next test tomorrow."

Nylora grunted but set Map Port on the ground.

Chapter 10
The Interrupted Second Task

Jack, Nana and all of the Silversparks, as well as Zully, were huddled up next to the fire that Granny had made with a flick of her wand. They were in the living room of the castle, all staring at the same thing: the Map Port. The map lay on the ground in front of them in the middle of all the floating couches and chairs.

"If you remember, Jinx, the second Test of Kindness is the Test of Hurt," Granny looked at Jinx. Jinx nodded.

"Are you ready, Jinx?" wondered Trix.

"Yep," Jinx whispered. Even though she was trying not to show it on the outside, on the inside she was trembling and her heart was beating fast. "I think I'm ready." Jinx had slept well the night before after successfully completing the first task. But, now that she was about to begin the next task, she was nervous again.

She went around the room giving and receiving hugs and kisses as well as a slobbery lick from Zully. Everyone said, "Bye," "I love you," or "Stay safe" or all three to Jinx. When she was finished, she gave one last look around the room then looked back at the map and said, "Mapoleodoo!" She was so loud that everyone in the entire castle could probably hear her. "Show me a hospital near Malunia!" Jinx requested of the map.

Immediately, a small ghost-like version of a large, white building labeled "HOSPITAL" in big letters rose from the map. Jinx tapped the building twice with her shimmering wand and jumped into the map.

Jinx landed in the hospital in the middle of a large crowd. However, no one seemed to have noticed her falling from the ceiling except for the child she landed on.

"Sorry," said Jinx cautiously, scared she may have hurt the child. Jinx quickly tucked her wand up her shirt sleeve. "Sorry," she said again to the young child.

"Like I'm just gonna accept your apology just like,"

the child snapped her fingers, “that! You fell on my head, monkey-head!” She growled at Jinx who was still on the floor and slowly scooching backwards away from the little girl.

The child had quickly stood up and was now bending over Jinx so far that her long, black hair tickled Jinx’s stomach and Jinx’s long, blond, and almost white, ponytail swept the floor.

“I said I was sorry, okay?” mumbled Jinx, struggling to her feet. Jinx stared into the child’s cold, beady, purple eyes and the child stared back at Jinx’s kind, beautiful, brown eyes. Jinx realized she was looking very far down. The child was only about a foot and a half tall. Suddenly, the pieces fit together in Jinx’s head: the rudeness, the black hair, the purple eyes, and the very small height. This was Shanna Beautywhirl, the elf who had tried to ruin her first test.

Jinx decided not to say anything and started squeezing her way through the crowd, but then an angry voice called, “Wait!” attracting many people’s attention. Jinx turned back to Shanna, but the moment she did, she regretted it, as Shanna was still very mad.

Shanna shouted at the surrounding staring people, “What are you all looking at, monkey-heads?!” Her attitude reminded Jinx very much of Lola’s mother,

Nylora.

Shanna turned to Jinx. “You owe me.”

“Why would I owe you?” asked Jinx.

“You fell on my head from using Map Port so...” started Shanna.

“How do you know I used Map Port?” asked Jinx sternly.

“Just a guess,” Shanna sneered. “Now get me my bwankie!” she inquired completely changing her voice from a rude, mean, and nasty one, to a mock-baby one.

“You’re not a baby, Shanna,” Jinx hissed, “even though you are the size of one!”

“Just do it, Jinx,” Shanna demanded.

“Do it yourself, Shanna Uglywhirl!” sneered Jinx.

“I’m injured, Jinx Silver-let-down!” Shanna hissed.

“Yeah, right!” Jinx laughed, starting to walk away.

Shanna placed herself in Jinx’s path and put her hands on her hips and squinted. “Come on! Get my bwankie. Don’t you have to help me? I’m hurt!”

“Fine!” Jinx grunted. “Where is this blanket?”

Shanna held onto Jinx's leg as she directed Jinx up a long, steep stair case. *Well, at least maybe I'll get the test done with,* Jinx thought as she was trying to think of something positive about being with Shanna. *But she might be trying to ruin the second test too,* worried Jinx.

They continued to climb stairs and every so often, Shanna would tap hard on Jinx's shin and say something like, "Hurry up, slow poke". When they finally got to the top of the stairs, Shanna directed Jinx through an uncrowded hallway.

"Stop!" said Shanna finally, as they passed an open room with a little boy getting his ears checked. "It's in there, in the back of the closet, on a shelf," she said directing Jinx to the door opposite the boy's room. Shanna jumped off Jinx's leg.

"Wait," said Jinx, "what are you doing?"

"I'm injured, remember? I can't go in there, I wouldn't be able to find-"

"You're not injured," Jinx sighed

"You fell on my head and I'm much smaller than you!" Shanna argued.

"Well, then how can you stand, walk, and hold onto my leg so long up those steep-ow!" Shanna's little elf body had somehow managed to purposely knock Jinx into the door behind her.

“How did you do that?” asked Jinx rubbing the new bump on her head.

“Magic,” said Shanna smirking.

“I’m not going in there,” said Jinx, pointing at the closed door behind her. Something about all of this really did not seem right to Jinx.

Shanna grunted. “Just do it!” she begged, continuously kicking Jinx’s feet.

Jinx felt like she had no choice and hoped that as soon as she got Shanna’s blanket, she could get rid of Shanna. So, she stood up, faced the door, hesitated, but slowly turned the knob not knowing that the evil elf was smirking behind her. Jinx peeked inside.

“Go in, go in,” urged Shanna holding in her evil cackles.

Each step Jinx took into the large closet, made her regret going with Shanna at all. After a few moments of walking like a zombie in the dark, Jinx said, “I don’t think there’s anything in here. Can you turn the light on?” But instead of hearing the soft clicking of a light switch, she heard the loud banging sound of a door being slammed shut. There was no longer any light in the closet at all. It was pitch black.

"Finally, we're alone together, Jinx," Shanna said no longer trying to hide the wickedness in her voice. "After my most honored assistant failed and a bunch of other elves failed as well as my special talking boliqua, I guess it was time that I get you myself."

"What do you mean?" questioned Jinx as she struggled to see.

But Shanna didn't answer, instead she said loudly and clearly, "This girl is a liar, I would like to shoot fire!" Only a tiny spark of fire shot out of her wand, illuminating the room so Jinx could easily see that the wand was shrinking by the second. Shanna continuously flicked the shrinking wand fiercely.

"Shoot fire!" Shanna demanded, her temper rising as fast as her wand was shrinking. "This girl is a liar; I would like to shoot fire!"

Fortunately for Jinx, yelling the spell did not help Shanna. In fact, this time nothing happened at all.

"AHHHHH!" screamed Shanna with frustration as Jinx struggled to get her own wand out of her sleeve. She was not quite sure what she was going to do with it as she had yet to learn any spells.

Shanna, with her skinny, shrinking wand and Jinx, with her beautiful shimmering wand, flicked furiously at each other. However, Shanna was too angry and frustrated and Jinx was too confused and a bit scared to know what to do.

Then suddenly, they both stopped; a large gust of wind was whooshing through the room, knocking Jinx to the ground, but Shanna, instead was lifted off the floor and held in the air, in the fog of the wind, only a few inches away from hitting her head on the low ceiling. Jinx watched as Shanna's shape changed before her eyes. Jinx instantly recognized the odd woman who had been at her house in the forest earlier that week. Then, there was a puff of dark, foggy smoke and Shanna, the odd woman or whoever she was disappeared.

"Shanna?" called Jinx, peering through the darkness trying to see with only a bit of fire and glowing magic dust.

There was no answer, as Jinx had expected. There was not even a sign of movement except the flickering of the fire and the dust and smoke drifting around the closet.

Chapter 11
The Battle against the Dark Side

BOOM! The smoke vanished as fast as you can snap your fingers and suddenly with a crack of thunder, a woman appeared in the closet directly in front of Jinx. The woman wore high heels that took her about three inches off the ground, although she was already much taller than an average woman. She wore a long, purple cape that dragged along behind her and she had a veil that attached to a black hat which sat on her black, wavy hair and covered her heavily made-up face so you could barely see the evil smile she wore on her red lips.

"Ma-wah-ha-ha-ha!" she cackled. "You might have hid from me for ten years, my dear girl, but there's no escaping this time!"

"Wa-Wa-Wazilma?" Jinx stuttered.

"That's right, my girl," Wazilma snorted, "smart one, aren't ya?"

"No," thought Jinx aloud. "You can't be Wazilma! You're Shanna in disguise and for a little bit you were disguised as that odd woman. How do you know the odd woman?"

"That's how anybody would transform. I'M NOT ODD!" screamed Wazilma.

"...and Shanna?"

"How else would I be the M.P.S.W.?"

__M__ost __P__owerful __S__orcerer in the __W__orld, thought Jinx.

"Ma-wa-ha-ha-ha-ha!" Wazilma cackled. "My elf body may be gone, but good for me as I also have a wizard body!"

"Well...we..." sputtered Jinx watching the wand in Wazilma's hand that had once shrunk, grow back to normal size. "I have more power than you."

"You don't know how to use it though, do you?" laughed Wazilma.

"Yeah, I do!" lied Jinx before she could stop herself.

"Then, come on, throw a spell at me," jeered

Wazilma.

Jinx just stood there, ashamed of herself.

"Looks like we've got that cleared up," said Wazilma.

Bang! Bang! Bang! Someone was at the door.

"Jinx, it's me!" called James. "I know you're in there! Whenever someone is taking a test we can follow them using Granny's Map Port. And, we can also detect when someone is using magic. It's okay. I used magic too when I was a kid. You'll get another chance to pass the second test tomorrow."

Jinx shifted into a hiding spot trying to inch herself to the door while keeping an eye on Wazilma for any spell she may cast, but fortunately Wazilma seemed to have hidden also.

Bang! Bang! Bang!

"Jinx there's no point hiding. I know you are in there and I know why. There's no reason to be ashamed! Come on!" Jinx twisted the door knob still keeping an eye out for Wazilma.

"Listen," said James, slipping past Jinx as the door flew open. "It's – Wazilma!" he shouted shocked to see the evil sorcerer.

"This girl is a liar; I would like to shoot fire!" shouted Wazilma, unexpectedly. This time a big blast of fire shot out of her wand right at Jinx, who dodged it by inches.

"That's the only spell you know, huh?" said Jinx bravely, not showing any sign of the fear bubbling inside of her.

Wazilma spat at her. James directed his wand at Wazilma and chanted, "Make the evil one freeze, just for a minute please." Wazilma instantly froze.

James immediately turned to Jinx and started to speak quickly, "Listen, carefully. I'm not even sure that spell will give us a whole minute. You have more power than me so you are going to have to learn this fast. To cast a spell, you think of something in your head, wave your wand twice above it and your wish will come true. However, for dark and more powerful spells, you must give your wand a flick and say anything that tells what you'd like to do. But, it must rhyme."

The room sat in silence while Jinx panicked trying to think of a spell. Just as Wazilma started to move, one came to her. "This is someone evil who we must end; with a wave of my wand, Sorson I will send!" Jinx shouted as she flicked her wand towards Wazilma. An arrow shot from the tip of Jinx's wand at Wazilma's chest. Wazilma quickly snapped her fingers and disappeared a split second before the arrow would have hit her.

"I'm surprised she still has enough power to do that," James panted. "Come on, we have to follow her."

"But, how?" Jinx asked.

"I think I know a way," said James as he pulled his Map Port out of his pocket. "Sometimes this works and you can see where certain sorcerers are if they have recently used magic." James then shouted, "Mapoleodoo! Where is Wazilma?"

A ghost-like image of Wazilma popped up in a field not far from Malunia. "There!" said James excitedly. He tapped on the image of Wazilma and he and Jinx jumped into Map Port.

"Where are we?" wondered Jinx staring at her surroundings.

"Wazilma's house, I'm guessing," replied James, glaring at a beautiful, yellow mansion in the distance.

"Wazilma has a house?" wondered Jinx.

"I guess. Right now, we need to catch up." And with that, James sprinted off after a small black figure moving fast across the massive garden with Jinx closely at his heels.

"Jinx! Jinx!"

Jinx turned around and saw Alexis, Trix, Lola, Nylora, Jack, Granny, Nana and even Zully about a hundred meters away. They each had wands in their hands, except Trix and Jack who stood closely behind the others. Zully had obviously been cursed again and now had vampire fangs that stuck out of her mouth.

Nylora moved first, except she ran toward the mansion. The rest followed Jinx and James.

Suddenly, Wazilma, still off in the distance, stopped, turned and started running towards them. When Wazilma got closer, she pointed her wand at them and screamed, "Kill the crowd, they are being too loud!" While she was determined and confident, nothing happened as Wazilma's wand had started to shrink again.

As Wazilma paused to study her shrinking wand, Zully who was ahead of the rest of the group took the advantage to bite her. Wazilma shot something out of her wand that caused Zully to let go. While Zully whimpered, Wazilma was able to disappear inside the mansion.

"Listen," said Granny to everyone, "we all came to help Jinx, but only one person here can really destroy Wazilma. Only one can really be the hero and she is the youngest sorcerer here with a wand. Jinx, I am sorry to put you under so much pressure, but you truly are the hero here. Use a powerful spell against her and aim the best you can!" Everyone looked at Jinx. She was shaking, but she nodded. She couldn't let the others down.

Just then, four scaly, large animals with wings swooped down from a balcony of the mansion flying towards them. As they came closer, it was apparent that they were dragons and they each carried a rider. One had Wazilma, one had Nylora and the other two dragons each carried an elf.

Before the dragons could shoot fire and before the sorcerers could cast spells, Jinx acted quickly. She pointed her wand at Wazilma's chest, up on the dragon where she had nowhere else to go. "This is someone evil who we must end; with a wave of my wand, to Sorson I will send!" she shouted. Jinx was confident, brave and determined and those three things were the keys to her outstanding power. The arrow hit Wazilma's chest and she fell off the dragon and disappeared.

Jinx had done it! She had been the hero. However, there was little time to celebrate now as there was still work to be done. She turned her wand on one of the dragons and announced, “The dragons are done; let them have no more fun!”

The spell bounced off each dragon and on to the next, killing each as it went. The dragons fell to the ground, squishing the three riders.

“There she is!” a pale bald elf shouted as he climbed out from under the dead dragon pointing at Jinx. “You defeated our master!”

“Kill her!” chanted Nylora as she crawled out from under her dragon. “Kill her, Gisheramit!”

“Mom!” cried Lola. “I can’t believe you! I always knew you had a secret!”

“Lola, meet Uncle Gisheramit and Uncle Gikamin!” sniggered Nylora.

“I like that spell you used there on our master, Jinx,” Gisheramit said evilly. Then, he quickly yelled, “This is someone evil who we must end; with a wave of my wand, to Sorson I will send!”

Jinx was faster though and just as an arrow shot out of his wand at Jinx, a large blast shot out of Jinx’s wand. It turned the arrow around and sent it the other way, directly back at Gisheramit, who vanished instantly. Jinx turned her aim towards the other elf,

Gikamin.

"Wait! Wait!" cried Gikamin. "I was born into the family. I didn't choose to be her most loyal assistant."

Jinx decided to come back to him later. She turned to Nylora. She hated to do this to Lola, even though she knew it was for the best. This time, she said it without determination, without bravery and without confidence. "This is someone evil who we must end; with a wave of my wand, to Sorson I will send." Nothing happened.

Lola walked over to Jinx. "Let me do it, Jinx. I can't believe this evil person is my mother. I know that I can say it confidently and bravely." Jinx backed away. Lola faced her mother and repeated the spell. Nylora disappeared.

Jinx turned her attention back to the other elf.

"Please!" Gikamin pleaded. "Please!"

"If you show me to my mother, I won't hurt you. But if you don't, you're done," Jinx threatened.

Gikamin sighed with relief. "Yes, of course."

"You guys go," said Jinx turning to her family. "I'll go get mom."

"She's my mom, too," said Trix.

"And my wife," reminded Jack.

"Okay," Jinx said to them. She turned to the rest of them. "We'll see you in Malunia!" They all disappeared.

"Come on," said Gikamin.

They followed the elf into the mansion where right in the entrance hall, Jinx's mother, Kate, was tied up, with her mouth taped shut.

"Mm mm mm!" Kate tried to speak.

Jinx took one look at her mom and quickly waved her wand twice over her head. The tape come off her mother's mouth and the ties came undone from around her. Jinx, Trix and Jack immediately hugged Kate, so happy that they were all speechless. They didn't even notice that the pale, bald elf called Gikamin snuck away.

Chapter 12
"What Just Happened?"

"What just happened?" was everyone's question in Malunia and it was Kate's too, no matter how many times Jinx explained the magical world to her mother.

The only people that really knew the answer to that question were Nana, Granny, Alexis, and James. And eventually they got tired of the questions so they posted a sign that read:

What Just Happened?

The Meeting

Are you one of the wonderers who keep wondering: "What just happened?" If you just answered, "yes", come to the meeting on January 26th in the Grand Park.

Maybe we will see you there,

Trinity Hazelpond (Nana)

Peachy Silverspark (Granny)

James Silverspark

Alexis Silverspark

January 26th arrived and hundreds of chairs were set up in the park for all of Malunia citizens. Alexis stood in front of the crowd.

"Okay," Alexis said into her microwand, which is what it is called when you turn your wand into a microphone. "We're going to start now." All of the Malunia citizens took their seats and looked up at Alexis.

"So," said James, who was standing on the stage next to Alexis, "believe it or not, this meeting is for someone who was there the entire time and that is our daughter, Jinx Silverspark. However, we decided to invite all of the citizens to listen so that any and all confusion can be explained." James turned towards Jinx, who was sitting in the front row and said, "Now, Jinx, you became the most powerful sorcerer in the world for one reason, one slightly confusing reason. That reason is that I am a wizard and your mother is a fairy. When we married and had you, you received all of each of our powers. If we had both been wizards or both been fairies, you would have received only the powers of a wizard or a fairy. It is very unusual to be born to a fairy and a wizard. Now, Wazilma was the M.P.S.W. We were not clear how she was so powerful for all of these years until you told us about Shanna. Obviously, Wazilma was also mixed like you, except she was half wizard and half elf. However, the reason you were more powerful than Wazilma is that fairies are more powerful than elves. Do you understand?"

Jinx nodded as this information was mostly what she expected.

James continued to speak. "What just happened was because Wazilma wanted to kill you because she loved being the Most Powerful Sorcerer in the World. That is what has kept her alive for the past 2,036 years. But, over the days since your 10th birthday, she has been losing power as you have been gaining power. Your mother, Kate, was kidnapped because Wazilma's assistant made a mistake and thought she was you." James paused again to look at Jinx who nodded. She had figured this much out, too.

"Jinx, you might wonder why Lola was with you in the non-magical world. Well, Nylora was Wazilma's spy who was working in the non-magical world. Wazilma had heard a rumor that Alexis and I had a baby, she knew that your powers would someday be stronger than hers. Nylora was spying on you and each week Nylora would pass the information Lola accidentally gave her on to Wazilma. However, Wazilma couldn't be sure it was you until you turned ten."

Jinx nodded again, as this too she had already guessed.

James continued, "You are the queen of Malunia now. And as queen, you have these guards." Jinx felt overwhelmed. She was only ten. How was she supposed to be a queen? But before she had too much time to think about this, two creatures Jinx had never seen before stepped forward towards her. They had snake like faces, manes like lions and eye like an owls. They stood on their furry hind legs wearing nothing but a necktie.

"These are zolbins and they have been put under the illegal talking spell, but don't worry, we have permission. They will report to you every week about Malunia. In fact, they should have their first report ready for you now and unfortunately they have some unexpected, terrifying news."

"I'm Bob," said the zolbin on the right in a low voice.

"And I'm Dimazeelama," said the other one.

Bob sniggered and Dimazeelama hit him in the face.

"We're still training them," murmured James to Jinx. "They might seem a bit out of control, but zolbins are extremely brave and loyal."

"So," Bob said, "we were hoping to give a good first report but –"

"-but we can't," interrupted Dimazeelama.

"We are sensing that danger is coming," said Bob, not blinking once.

"Wazilma's great, great, great, great, great and on and on, granddaughter is angry with you. Wazilma's follower, Gikamin, has apparently tracked her down and informed her that you killed her grandmother. She wants revenge and she will do whatever she can do to get it." And with that, the zolbins disappeared into a mist leaving the town of Malunia gasping and Jinx with thousands of butterflies fluttering their wings and dancing in her stomach.

Chapter 13
H.E.A.

Jinx woke up early the next morning after a series of dreadful nightmares. In the most recent nightmare, Jinx had been chased and killed by Wazilma's great, great, great, great, great, and on and on granddaughter and she only awoke when she reached heaven. *It was just a dream,* Jinx persuaded herself. *Or the future,* said another part of her.

Jinx sat in darkness for a while. She looked over at Lola who was still asleep beside her. She didn't illuminate her room with her wand but stayed in the darkness until sunlight peeked in through her long curtains. She blinked a few times before her eyes adjusted to the sudden light. The butterflies in her stomach remained where they were. After the meeting ended yesterday with the zolbins report, everyone in Malunia was worried about the future. Jinx and her family had returned to the castle to start planning, but had not had many ideas. The only thing Jinx was sure of at that meeting was that Lola was to always live with Jinx's family, whether it was in Malunia or in her other home in the woods.

Thinking about the new queen job she had only just heard about, and worrying about Wazilma's granddaughter, Jinx walked out to her balcony to take a look at her town. As she looked out at the beautiful town of Malunia, a clump of balloons floated up towards her. She reached out and caught two of them. One said: CONGRATULATIONS! And the other one said: COME JOIN THE PARTY OUTSIDE THE CASTLE!

Jinx let the balloons fly away and some of the butterflies seemed to go with them. Jinx had no idea what they were celebrating, but was never one turn down a party.

Jinx quickly woke Lola up and the two of them entered the glass box and urged it down. When it finally hit the ground of the first floor, she burst open the big doors at the entrance of the castle to reveal almost all of Malunia's citizens dancing around and having a good time. Jinx was surprised considering most of them had probably heard by now that Wazilma's great, great, great and so on, granddaughter wanted revenge. But, they seemed to have forgotten that for the moment. Jinx was excited to see the party and happily joined the crowd, leaving thoughts of revenge behind her.

"You came, Jinx, you came!" Nana said excitedly as she flew not far away from Jinx's nose. "We've got time to worry about the next battle later. It's important to take time to celebrate and be happy when you can!" Nana landed on Jinx's shoulder, soared about a foot into the sky, did a backflip and then landed gently back on her shoulder. "Fly, Jinx!" she said.

"What do you mean?" wondered Jinx.

"Well," Nana started to explain, settling herself comfortably onto Jinx's shoulder, "when fairies are completing their tests they have to be enlarged and they also have to hide their wings if they go into the nonmagical world like you did. It is a tradition that fairies are returned to their tiny size when they have finished their tests. But as you know, you are only half fairy, so you are not small. It is also a tradition that this is the first time a fairy flies."

"What do you mean 'when they have finished their tests'? I haven't finished mine."

"Oops! I may have said too much! You'll see later," said Nana. "But now, just fly!"

"How?"

"Flap your wings and look at the sky, of course," said Nana as though it should be obvious.

Jinx flapped her wings eagerly and stared at the sky, trying hard to concentrate.

"Flap faster," suggested Nana. Jinx flapped her wings harder and faster.

"Now, push off with your feet," Nana instructed.

Jinx followed Nana's directions and she was suddenly off the ground. Many people looked around and cheered and clapped for Jinx whose feet dangled several feet off the ground. While the crowd watched, Jinx took off into the air, did a couple of flips she had learned from watching Nana and settled back down near the ground. Jinx gave a huge smile. Flying was amazing! She had never felt so free.

Just then, Jinx caught sight of Granny squeezing through the crowd. She climbed on a stage that had just magically appeared and said "Hello," into her microwand. The fluttering fairies, powerful wizards and all of the elves turned and gave their attention to

Granny.

"As you might know, I am Jinx Silverspark's wizard grandmother," Granny began. A few sorcerers turned back to glance at Jinx, who had settled herself back on the ground. "And I am proud to announce," continued Granny, "my granddaughter has passed the Fairy Tests of Kindness and the Wizard Tasks of Danger!"

The citizens of Malunia clapped and cheered, but all Jinx could do was smile.

"Please, come to the stage, Jinx," said Granny. Jinx easily made her way through the crowd as everyone stepped aside to give her room.

"How?" asked Jinx as she stood next to Granny on the stage.

"Well, you completed the Fairy Test of Poverty by helping the family in the treehouse," Granny said into the microwand. "By saving your mother, Kate, you completed the Test of the Hurt, even though you needed a little bit of magic to do it. By inviting Lola to always live with you, you completed the Test of the Lonely. And, by defeating Wazilma, you completed the Tasks of Danger that were much more difficult than the actual wizard tasks. You were both as kind and brave as a fairy and wizard need to be."

The crowd clapped and cheered. Jinx screamed with delight. And they all lived **H**appily **E**ver **A**fter.

Epilogue

Bob: “Did that just end in **H**appily **E**ver **A**fter?”

Dimazeelama: “I know, right?”

Bob: “After we just told them that Wazilma’s great, great, great, great, great, great, great, great, great, great...”

Dimazeelama: “Zzzzzzzz....”

Bob: “...great, great, great, great, great...”

Dimazeelama: “Zzzzzzzz....”

Bob: “...great, great, great, great, great...”

Dimazeelama: “Zzzzzzzz....”

Bob: "…great granddaughter wants revenge! They are going to throw a party! Wake up, Dimazeelama!"

Dimazeelama: "Uh!!!"

Bob: "We need to immediately start planning! Queen Jinx is going to need us."

ABOUT THE AUTHOR

Cara Newman is originally from Michigan, but currently resides in Bangkok, Thailand with her parents and younger brother and sister. She is a fourth grade student attending the International School Bangkok where she enjoys playing sports such as soccer, basketball and tennis. She also enjoys dancing and spending time with friends. When she has free time, she loves to read and write. Her favorite books at the moment are the Harry Potter series by J.K. Rowling. *Jinx* is Cara's second novel. Her first novel, *Travel Bracelets,* was published in 2014.

Made in the USA
Lexington, KY
13 February 2017